I0788406

Jackie the Beanstalk

A fractured fairy tale

Other Titles by Nathan Everett

STEVEN GEORGE & THE DRAGON

STEVEN HAS ALWAYS known he was a dragonslayer, but on the day his village sends him to slay the fearsome beast he realizes he doesn't know what a dragon looks like, where it lives, or how to kill it. His quest is facilitated by the exchange of "once-upon-a-times" with the people he meets on the endless road. Think Grimm. For young adults, not children.

A PLACE AT THE TABLE

THOUGH THE AMERICA Liam Cyning lives in is quite similar to the America of half a century or more ago, it is also fundamentally different. Ten clearly defined classes are the underpinning of American Society, determined by the educational system. As a newly assigned member of the Leader class, Liam is still uncertain what his role and responsibilities are. This story is a Bildungsroman, a literary genre that focuses on the psychological and moral growth of Liam Cyning from youth to adulthood.

CITY LIMITS

WHO AM I, really? It's a common question. It's part of being self-aware. But is it important? Are we really nothing more than our accumulated lifetime of memories? Or is there something inside that makes us inherently who we are? Stripped of his memories and identity, Gee Evars must come to grips with who he is as he attempts to make a home among strangers by simply doing the right thing. *City Limits* is the story of Gee's loss of memory and the life and love he gains.

WILD WOODS

WHEN GEE EVARS wandered into town, he lost his memory in a daring rescue of a toddler in the raging Rose River. Now the man without a memory has become a force that even the Families need to reckon with. When the city votes to annex South Rosebud, Gee accompanies a small army of high school students to tear down the fence that has separated the cultivated hickory Forest from the Wild Woods. This is where the sequel to the popular novel *City Limits* begins. Gee and his crew must find a way to tame the Wild Woods, uncover its secrets, and live to tell the story. Gee's real work in Rosebud Falls has just begun.

THE GUTENBERG RUBRIC

TWO RARE-BOOK LIBRARIANS race across three continents to find and preserve a legendary book printed by Johannes Gutenberg. Behind them, a trail of bombed libraries draws Homeland Security to launch a worldwide search for biblio-terrorists. Keith and Maddie find love along the way, but will they survive to enjoy it?

FOR MONEY OR MAYHEM

COMPUTER FORENSICS DETECTIVE Dag Hamar has been hired to help a credit card company beef up network security, but are his new co-workers helping him or attacking him? Security video doesn't lie, does it? Dag is about to get dragged from behind his computer screen—away from the comparative safety of cyberspace—into the dirty streets of Seattle where an online predator has become a real-life serial kidnapper. But will he be in time to save his new romance and the daughter who is a victim.

FOR MAYHEM OR MADNESS

COMPUTER FORENSICS DETECTIVE Dag Hamar is on the case again! In this sequel to *For Money or Mayhem*, Dag is commissioned by the Financial Crimes Enforcement Network (FinCEN) to find and stop a dangerous hacker who appears to be a credible threat to national security. Follow Dag as he erases his own digital identity and goes on the trail around the world to track down and neurtralize Hacker X before he does something really dangerous like erase all the nuclear launch codes in the world. Or maybe, Dag should help him.

FOR BLOOD OR MONEY

DAG HAMAR IS a hard-boiled computer forensics detective with all the trimmings: the Seattle Waterfront office, the sexy young assistant who adores him, and an attitude to match the constant gray drizzle outside his window. And a new missing person case. The only problem is he's a middle-aged computer geek who doesn't do missing persons. And the only clue he has is the missing man's laptop. Dag Hamar and Deb Riley discover hidden files and computer code can be as dangerous as dark alleys and flying bullets as they enter the high-stakes game of of tracing a missing friend and the billion-dollar fortune that disappeared with him.

MUNICIPAL BLONDES

COMPUTER FORENSICS DETECTIVE Deb Riley has been cut loose to continue the work of her partner, Dag Hamar. He sent her to get the code from a dead man's tattoo. He told her she needed to crack the encryption on Simon's thumb drive. He told her he loved her. And then he died. Now Deb finds she is in possession of something everyone wants and will do anything to get. Including kill her.

Enter the world of Deb Riley, code breaker, detective, and master of disguise, as she races into the heart of the mystery and risks discovery or worse. She has Dag's reputation to live up to.

STOCKS & BLONDES

COMPUTER FORENSICS DETECTIVE Deb Riley is on the case again, this time with a dead woman named Georgia and a house full of computers. Georgia's father doesn't believe the police finding that she committed suicide. He's sure there was foul play involved. He had no idea how foul it was. Hacking into the computers starts a deadly game as neighbors, friends, and even Georgia, prove not to be what they appear to be. Infiltrating the cabal throws Deb into her deepest disguise ever. Worse, it puts her in danger of ending up just like Georgia.

THE VOLUNTEER

JOURNEY INSIDE THE head of a chronically homeless man--a man that in a less politically correct age we might have called a hobo. Gerald Good, known now only as G2, volunteered to take the place of a homeless man, believing he would work his way back quickly. Ten years later, twenty... thirty years, find G2 alone in his head, his memories, and his boxcar.

ISBN 978-1-955874-09-0

Designed by Nathan Everett

Cover photo by Evgenyrichko, ID 732180235 licensed from Shutterstock.com

Divider art by Aleks47, ID 143768332 licensed from Shutterstock.com

Printed in the United States of America

Jackie the Beanstalk

A fractured fairy tale

NATHAN EVERETT

ELDER ROAD BOOKS
LYNNWOOD WA

Chapter 1

Cap and Gown

BEFORE WE GET STARTED, I might as well tell you, I'm a girl. I'm eighteen and tall and thin. I like sports, outdoors stuff like camping, and animals. Pop—my Grandpa—started calling me a beanstalk years ago when I started growing—up, not out. He said I was a real tomboy, too. Mam—Grandma—said I needed to grow tall just to contain all the good in me. I love Grandma Mam. She always has something kind to say about everything. Aunt Misty just said it meant I was strong and empowered—a real woman. I thought in any case, it would have been nice to have tits by the time I graduated from high school. Wasn't to be.

Did you know thesaurus.com lists 385 synonyms for 'beanstalk.' And nearly every one applies to me. Angular, slender, gangly, skinny, lanky, lean... You get the idea. I'm a tall, gangly, sometimes uncoordinated, pile of bones with a thin layer of meat and skin pulled over the top. I'm a scrawny, rawboned broomstick with a soaring attitude to match my statuesque height. You get the picture, right? I'm tall and skinny. But what the thesaurus doesn't mention is that I'm deceptively strong from playing basketball, disk golf, soccer, volleyball, and track. And I have a wicked arm when I'm throwing a softball.

I wear my basketball varsity letter, but I lettered in four different sports.

Being the kind of curious kid I've always been, I looked up 'beanstalk' in the urban dictionary of slang, too, and I found two completely different (in my opinion) definitions.

1) Being a plain annoying human being.

2) Someone doing something legendary.

I suppose I could be legendarily annoying and fit both definitions. Of course, those are just the top definitions. I like the last one on the page just as much.

3) The epitome of clitoral arousal. A clit erection. As in 'Lick my beanstalk!'

Well, you get the idea. So, how tall is tall? Not *that* tall if you're a guy. I'm 6'3". If you want that in metric, I'm 190.5 centimeters. How skinny? 133 pounds naked. Not many have seen that, yet. Dan Blackwell saw most of it back when... Well, you know. Oh, yeah. That's 60 kilos. I'd be worth a fortune if I was cocaine. Yeah, baby. Like $1.8 million. In the right market. A lot more than I'm worth as a tall skinny girl. I'd have to play in the WNBA for, like, ten years to earn that much. So, I guess I won't be getting rich any time soon.

I've lived with Mam and Pop since I was eleven. And Aunt Misty. She was just graduating from high school when I moved in. She never moved out. I got my mother's old room. My parents? Don't ask. We never talk about them. Looking at Mom's room when I moved in, though, you'd never think she was the kind of person she turned out to be. I quickly adopted Misty's words for her parents and they became Mam and Pop to both of us. It was so much easier than keeping track of whether we were referring to my grandparents or her parents. Might not be the same as everyone, but it made Misty and me feel even more like sisters.

Okay, a little bit of the backstory. Did you ever notice how country songs sung by men are all, like, "Hot girls in teeny tiny shorts, I will make you my wife, bear my children, front porch, family values, and casseroles." Oh yeah, and "Poor me, my truck ran away with my dog." While country songs sung by women are, like, "Oops! I killed my husband." Well, now you get an idea about my dad and mom. She's got another fourteen years before she's eligible for parole.

Poor Mam and Pop were in their late fifties and thinking about retirement and maybe traveling around the world as soon as they could get Misty out of the house. Then I moved in. Now, they're pushing seventy and still haven't retired. Still hoping the youngest will move out so they can start traveling. I probably will, but I hate to leave Misty. She's more like a big sister than an aunt. Maybe she'll move with me. Oh, wow! The trouble we could get into together would be epic!

Not that I ever get into trouble, mind you. It's just an expression. Sort of.

Like I couldn't find a date for senior prom because Dan Blackwell already got Randi Bishop preggers, so he wasn't going to take me. So, I bought a couple's ticket and got Misty to go with me. It was easier for me to get a tux than a formal, so Misty got to wear the gown and go as my date. Mam about had a coronary when she saw my haircut. Slicked back and parted on the side. When she saw me in the living room in my tux and my neatly pasted on pencil-thin mustache, she thought I was my date. Oops!

Misty is almost a foot shorter than me, so we made a striking pair on the dance floor. It was almost halfway through the prom before anybody figured out who it was. You wouldn't believe the number of guys who hit on my aunt. Or, for that matter, the number of girls who hit on me.

I kept my hair short and really look butch now. Not that I'm that way. I'd like some guy to get sweet on me. I'm just not interested in spending the effort to tame one. Probably end up like my mother. Misty, on the other hand, is very feminine and cute. Unfortunately, she depended on that in life and wasn't that successful. She's worked at Starbucks ever since she graduated. So, don't go believing the tall tales you hear about the flirty barista who is suddenly swept off her feet by the rich handsome billionaire, or something. Misty's still pulling shots. Maybe she set the bar a little high.

So, where's this story going, anyway? Hell if I know. So, sometimes I'll just talk to fill the void. I'd say it actually started at commencement. When I accepted my diploma from Principal Rogers, he looked up at me—short guy— and took my hand so we could shake for the photographers. Only in that minute, I could have walked around the entire stadium and counted every one of the two thousand people present. As they say, time stood still.

"I expect I'll hear news of your great accomplishments, Jackie. You have a unique future before you. I've put your travel documents in your folder. Make us proud," he said. Only it was like his voice was somewhere far away, even though I could see his lips moving, a little out of sync with what I was hearing. It was like his voice was on the other side of some canyon or something. Yeah, Mrs. Donahue would say the right word was 'chasm.' He spoke to me across a great chasm complete with an eerie echo. I paid attention in school. Then the camera flash went off and I walked off the platform—one of 300 students in my graduating class.

I'D LIKE TO say that was the weirdest thing that ever happened to me, but weirdness kind of follows me around like a lost puppy. Take that time soon after I got my driver's license, for instance. I was driving Pop's old Ford Fairlane 500. I know. Sounds weird already, but Pop bought the car new in '68 with money he'd saved all through high school. Then he was drafted and spent four years as a jungle rat in Southeast Asia. The car still only had a couple thousand miles on it at the time and so he just kept it in the garage and used some of his military pay to buy a motorcycle. Well, I won't get into how he met Mam and packed her off on an around-the-USA motorcycle trip and they got back with my mom in the hopper and a smile on their faces.

But that's how the fifty-some-year-old car happened to be in the garage when I decided to go shopping with Misty. I mean, Misty never learned to drive and never really went anywhere more than a bicycle ride away unless someone else was driving. She said driving was what boys were for, but she was happy enough when I offered to drive. She's still a kid at heart and filled with delusions. We'd gone to the mall, had burgers at Wendy's, and were headed back home. I decided to stay off the main roads because I wasn't sure the Fairlane would go at freeway speeds even though it was in immaculate condition. I couldn't remember it having been out of the garage in the past five years, though it had current plates. But we were driving along without a care in the world when this voice says, "Turn right at the next corner."

All echoey like Principal Rogers' voice I told you about. I won't re-explain that. I looked over at Misty and she was just sitting there like she didn't hear a thing, the brat. I'm not crazy, so when I got to the next intersection I turned right. I was listening for further instructions, which weren't forthcoming, when I saw a dog in the middle of the road. I pulled to a stop and jumped out of the car, even though Misty was hollering "Be careful. Don't let it bite you."

Well, this poor mangy mutt wasn't interested in biting. He wanted to lick me half to death. Faker. He got up and followed me to the car and when I opened the door, he climbed in the back seat and lay down like he owned it.

And that's how I came to own Roadkill. Clever name, right? It's also how I came to have three months of duty pulling the Fairlane out of the garage every Saturday morning and washing it, then vacuuming out the inside and using some of that 'new car smell' polish to go over all the plastic and vinyl in the car and leather conditioner for the seats. After three months, Pop declared the car free of the mangy dog smell at last.

Weird, huh?

But that dog never leaves my side except when I go to school. Hardly even had to train him, except to get him to stand still while I gave him a bath. Now, he even tolerates a ribbon in his hair if I get in a mood.

MILE 0

WHERE WAS I?

Commencement was over and I found Mam, Pop, Misty, and Roadkill waiting for me outside the stadium so we could take family pictures with me in my graduation gown and holding tight to my diploma. I never opened it up. They'd mail the diploma sometime this summer. I knew all they gave us at commencement was an empty folder. And travel documents? I wanted to figure out what these 'travel documents' were that Principal Rogers mentioned but decided I should do that in private. Then Pop did something I never in a million years would have imagined. He held up the keys to the Fairlane and dangled them in front of my face. He pointed across the parking lot where that red and black fastback was sitting with a bow tied to the radio antenna.

"It's yours now. Drive it like you own it," he said. Oh, I gave him the biggest, crushingest hug you can imagine and a kiss right on his cheek. Then I did the same to Mam, only I had to bend over a lot farther to reach her cheek. I turned to Misty and grabbed her hand and took off running toward the car, my cap and gown flying and Roadkill barking at our heels. The three of us piled into the car and I started up the 390 Thunderbird Special V-8 engine and felt the Fairlane come to life beneath my fingertips.

"Where are we going?" Misty asked. Always the practical one.

"I don't know. Principal Rogers said my travel documents were in my diploma folder." I handed it to her and a packet of papers fell out, including an old-fashioned AAA TripTik. How weird can things get? Like, was this all a scheme he cooked up with Pop? Old car and a really old map.

"It starts here," Misty said, pointing helpfully at the first page.

"Okay. Write down the odometer reading: 0. You think that can be real? Has it tipped over once or twice?" I asked.

Probably never know the answer to that one. I revved the engine a little to feel it rumble. "You're my GPS, girl. Let's see where this map takes us." I pushed the four-on-the-floor into first, only chirped a little when I let out the clutch, and pulled out of the stadium parking lot following Misty's instructions to turn right. We were on the road.

MILE 93

WE'D BEEN DRIVING along for almost two hours, getting up over the mountain pass and singing 60s songs at the top of our lungs. Sometimes Roadkill joined in as if he knew the music. It was different when he started to whine, though.

"Hey, does my guy need a bathroom stop? Hmm. Me, too. Watch for a place where we can pull over," I said.

"Um... The TripTik says 'Diner on right.' It should be... There it is!"

I saw it in time to pull into the gravel parking lot and find a parking spot. I jumped out of the car and grabbed Roadkill's leash, then saw some plastic baggies on the seat. Knew what those were for. I grabbed one and headed for the grass out back.

"Hey, see if you can find some water for him," I called to my aunt. At this moment, she was really more like my sidekick than an aunt. She was only seven years older than me. And we were having too much fun, just letting the old car run. Misty grabbed Roadkill's dish out of the back and disappeared into the diner. Roadkill did his business and I dropped it in a dumpster on my way to the front door. Misty appeared and said to come on in. "With Roadkill?"

"They said it was fine. I've got the three of us a booth." Well, I'd never heard of a diner that allowed dogs in, but indeed, Misty waved me to a booth.

"Wow! I'm starved. Why is everybody looking at me?" I asked.

"Probably because you're still wearing your cap and gown and all those things dangling around your neck," she laughed. "You could take it off." I started to panic.

"I can't," I squeaked. "I'm only wearing underwear."

"You wicked girl!" Misty laughed.

"That means I don't have my wallet either. Do you have any money?"

"I've got some money and I've got your wallet, too. Remember? You gave it to me before we left the house this afternoon."

"Well, thank goodness for that. I suppose I could take off some of the decorations," I said. I got to considering what I must look like. I mean, it was fine when I was surrounded by 300 others who looked the same. But in a diner in the middle of nowhere, it had to look pretty strange. The gown and mortarboard were dark, almost iridescent blue. My tassel and the shiny stole were silver. Those were the school colors. The stole only came down to the middle of my torso with pointy ends making like a beacon to show how far it was to the ground. Then there were the cords. Not to brag, but I was a pretty good student and active in all kinds of things. I had a white cord for having done 100 hours of community service projects. The light blue cord was because I was an AP scholar. The gold cord indicated that I graduated with a 3.5 GPA or better. Then on the left breast—if I had anything there—I had my athletic badge, a silver interlinked WW for West Wilford, with a flaming basketball cutting across it to indicate my principal varsity sport. We got little badges beneath that indicated the number of years we participated in each sport. I had fifteen badges. I guess I looked the part of a high-achieving grad.

The waitress took our orders and brought me the biggest, messiest chili burger I'd ever seen. There was a mountain of fries next to it. Misty had a chef salad. She might have thought it was going to be a sensible lo-cal meal, but the bowl it came in was the size of a regular serving bowl and I could see it was totally drenched in blue cheese dressing—Misty's favorite. The waitress even brought Roadkill a bowl of water and some kibble.

We were apparently in the vanguard of the dinner rush, because people started coming in and getting seated. Our waitress was hustling her butt off. I made a note to be real nice when I tipped her. I didn't want her to lose that butt. It was way too nice. I notice that kind of thing. Everybody who came in seemed to stop and look at me, then smile and nod. I guess that pride people have in graduates is present, even when they don't know them.

I don't know how we managed to finish our meal—aside from a few French fries and a little chunk of burger I slipped to Roadkill. I was mopping up the remains of the chili on my plate with a fry. Misty had done pretty well with her salad, too. I don't know how she manages to stay so cute and trim with as much as that girl eats. Course, people say the same about me, except for the cute part. We were just trying to decide if we wanted to split a sundae when we heard a ruckus at the cash register and looked up to see what was going on.

Some guy in a winter parka, gloves, and a ski mask was hassling the cashier. He was dressed way too warm for the weather. It was mid-June and the temp was just beginning to cool from the afternoon high of 75. A man in the booth nearest to the cashier started to get up and the fellow at the counter swung around and landed a blow on the side of his head with what was quickly obvious as a gun.

"The rest of you just sit down and shut up!" he yelled waving the gun around. "I'm just getting a take-out and some cash. So, take out all your cash and put it on your table. This pretty waitress is going to come around and collect it for me." He smacked my waitress on her butt— that fine butt I was noticing earlier—and prodded her forward with his gun. I saw the cashier reach for something and apparently the robber saw her, too. He swung back to her and fired. The cashier staggered back and hit the floor.

I honest to God do not know what came over me. He shot the cashier and slapped the butt of *my* waitress. I snatched the mortarboard off my head and used one of my best disk golf throws to launch it at the bastard. He never saw it coming as it lodged in the front of his throat. He dropped the gun, tried to take a step toward the door, and fell to the floor.

Roadkill was off like a flash, standing on him and growling. Then he sniffed at the guy, grabbed my cap, and trotted back to me. The guy didn't move, but a big puddle of blood collected under his neck.

Oh, shit! What had I done?

A WOMAN DECLARING herself a doctor, scurried around the counter to check on the cashier. She totally ignored the bleeding robber. I guess dead robber was more like it. I just stood there staring at what I'd done as two guys moved to search the perp. My waitress stepped up to our table and gently took the cap from Roadkill. She used her table rag that she washed all the tables with to wipe the blood off the corner of the mortarboard, carefully making sure it was clean. Then she placed it back on my head and made sure the tassel was hanging correctly. I just stared at her as she leaned forward and put a soft kiss right on my lips.

"Thank you, Warrior Wizard," she whispered. Then she cleared our plates as if nothing had happened. I looked after her sexy butt for a second and then looked at Misty to see what she thought. Her eyebrows were stuck somewhere up under her hairline and her mouth was at least as wide open as mine.

Just then another guy approached our booth. He laid a wallet, some change and the gun on our table.

"He didn't have much, I guess, but there's some cash in the wallet. It's all yours now." He turned and went back to the front where he and the other guy who'd searched the robber picked him up and dragged the body outside. A minute later, I heard the clang of the dumpster lid.

My waitress was back with two absolutely huge hot fudge sundaes that she put in front of Misty and me, and a little dish of ice cream for Roadkill. At least she knew not to put chocolate on the dog's dessert.

"How's the cashier?" I asked.

"The doctor said she'll be fine. He wasn't really aiming when he shot her and the bullet passed through without much damage. Don't worry about her. Your meal's been taken care of. If you want anything else, just say so. Coffee with your dessert?" Misty and I both nodded our heads and looked at each other.

"What the fuck just happened?" I whispered.

"If I believed what I saw, I'd say a guy tried to rob the diner, you killed him, and then everything went back to being normal. But that couldn't be right. Right?"

"Right. Um… This sundae is really good, though."

WE HUNG AROUND, expecting the state police or county sheriff or at least an ambulance to show up, but nothing seemed to be happening and no one seemed to expect anything to happen. I looked at Misty and she shrugged, so we stood to leave.

"What do we do with this stuff?" I asked.

"I guess you are supposed to take it," Misty said. I picked up the wallet and looked in it. There were some small bills and a fifty. I put the big bill on the table as a tip for our sexy waitress and then tossed the wallet to Misty.

"Put this and the gun in your bag. I don't have any pockets or a belt or anything."

"I don't see how you could need it as long as you have your cap and gown," Misty said. "Wicked!"

On the way to the door, people nodded our direction, Roadkill padding along behind us with his leash in his mouth. I carried his dishes. Our waitress met us at the door with a bag.

"The cook packed a breakfast for you. We don't know where your journey will take you, but we're glad it included our little diner." She presented me with the bag and then leaned in to stretch up on her toes and kiss me again. Only this was a really really good kiss. I'd be able to taste that kiss for the next couple of hours good. "Thank you, Warrior Wizard. Blessings on your travels."

We headed out to the Fairlane. Roadkill got in the back seat. I started the car, and felt the engine rumble to life. I took another look around before I pulled out of the parking lot to make sure no police were coming to arrest me. It looked like everyone in the diner had come outside to wave goodbye, my waitress in the lead. I hit the gas and popped the clutch. We peeled out of the parking lot onto the open road and were gone.

"Hi ho, Silver, away!" I shouted out. Misty started laughing.

Chapter 2

Crossing Denial River

MILE 147

"YOU THINK I'm my mother's daughter?" I asked Misty as we drove down the twisting road along a river. It bothered me. I just killed some hombre—I think. Maybe I should be in the cell next to my mother. How could people just ignore that and not even call the cops?

"Honey, you're asking the wrong person. My sister is fifteen years older than me. By the time I knew who she was, she was married and living two states away. And I didn't know her husband at all, so I couldn't tell you if he deserved killing like that bastard back at the diner. I know Mam and Pop weren't that surprised," Misty said. She reached over and patted my thigh.

No flashing red lights had come tearing up behind us, so I was guessing nobody cared about the guy I offed. Still couldn't believe I killed him with my mortarboard. At least I think I killed him. I never actually examined the body. Maybe it was all a set up.

"Well, I wiped most of that from my memory. Maybe someday a therapist worth her wage will dissect my brain and discover what kind of childhood I had. I really don't care much anymore. About either of them," I said.

I looked at the twisting river off the side of the road. Seemed like it was getting significantly bigger as we traveled. "I'm sure I remember some town along here that Mam and Pop took us to so we could see the Christmas decorations. Are we still on the same road?"

"There's no town marked on the map along here," Misty replied. "Looks like we cross the river in a couple of miles and continue on the other side. But no town."

"Well turn up the radio. Let's find out what station we're listening to."

We rode on and found the bridge. It looked like a pretty nice and fancy bridge to be out here in the wilderness like this. Even had streetlights marking it.

"Now this is just too strange," I said. "Who puts a bridge in the middle of nowhere with streetlights on it?"

"Oh, what was that story? The one where the kids climb in the closet and come out in a different world. There was a lamppost there."

"*The Lion, the Witch, and the Wardrobe*. We are not in Narnia. My head can't accept that. There must be some more logical explanation."

"Yeah. How about if there's a troll who lives under the bridge and he likes to be able to see what he's eating," Misty giggled.

"Oh, thanks a lot. That image will haunt my dreams. You're gross!" We laughed and kept driving, but I yawned pretty powerfully. "Do you think maybe we should find a hotel or something for the night? I'm getting tired."

"You think?" Misty asked. It took a second before I figured she was responding to the idea of needing a place to stay. "The TripTik says turn left and go to campsite 33."

"You're kidding. Turn where?"

"There!"

I slewed the car around and just barely made the corner into a campground I never even saw a sign for. I wasn't sure what good a campground was going to do us when what I wanted was a nice hot bath and a hotel bed.

"You could have given me more warning!" I yelled as I started looking for the campsite. Being told to camp here seemed just as normal as anything else that happened today. I was still hoping to see a Holiday Inn at the campsite. These were my travel documents Misty was reading from. I probably had a reservation.

"I swear it didn't say anything about a campsite when I was looking at the bridge location," she pouted. "Over there. That's site 33." I pulled into the campsite and stopped the car. The campsite had the same logo on it that I wore on my gown. WW with a flaming basketball. *Fuck!*

I got out of the car and stretched. It was actually a pretty comfortable ride, but too long in one position makes me crazy. Roadkill jumped out of the backseat and found a place to relieve himself before he even started sniffing around. Didn't blame him for that. I spied a washhouse just a little ways away.

"I'm headed for the girls' room," I called to Misty.

"Okay. I'll get some water for Roadkill. Whole campground looks deserted."

"Well, keep an eye out just in case." I wasn't sure I knew in case of what. I wasn't expecting to have to throw my hat at some phantom rapist or anything. Course, I didn't expect to do that the first time. I gathered up my robes and perched myself above the stool. Place looked clean enough, but why take chances with your butt? I had all kinds of images of rattlesnakes or something coming up out of the toilet. I got done quick and went out to wash my hands. There was even hot water in the faucets. I looked around and saw shower stalls with actual doors on them—not just a plastic curtain. I guessed maybe I was overreacting to the idea in my head about snakes.

I left the washroom and nearly stepped on one.

I screamed and the snake slithered away. I know, it was probably more afraid of me than I was of it, but I could scream louder. Roadkill and Misty reached me at a dead run.

"What is it? What happened?" Misty gasped. Roadkill started sniffing around.

"A snake. That's all. Just scared the shit out of me."

"Didn't you do that in the toilet?" Misty said. Roadkill rubbed up against me. "Well, while I'm down here, I'll empty the bladder, too. Um..."

"Roadkill and me'll wait here for you," I said. She smiled and nodded.

A few minutes later, she came out looking much refreshed. "Hot water!" she said happily.

"I figure I'll make use of the shower in the morning," I agreed as we walked back up to the campsite.

"Uh... Do we have a blanket or anything?" Misty asked. It was cooling off here in the foothills and we put our arms around each other as we walked.

"Not that I know of," I said. "Pop always keeps an emergency kit in the trunk of his Fusion. Maybe there's one in the Fairlane. I think we could put the back seat down and open the hatch. We might have enough room to lie down and Roadkill can keep us warm." We reached the campsite and Misty went to brush off the picnic table and pace around. I unlocked the hatchback and looked inside. "Misty? Did you do this?"

"Do what, hon?" She came around to look in the back. Roadkill put his front feet up on the opening so he could see in, too. The back was packed tight with everything I could think of that we'd need. There were sleeping bags, pillows, a tent, camp stools, a cooler, two huge backpacks, and my teddy bear. Don't laugh. A girl needs something nice and soft to cuddle up to at night and all I had was a teddy bear. "I guess we get to camp out," Misty said. She looked at me as if I had all this planned. I just shrugged my shoulders and looked right back at her shrugging hers.

We went about making camp, setting up the tent, and putting things away inside. Then Roadkill came up to me dragging a dead tree limb behind him.

"I don't think we can play fetch with that," I said. "But we could build a fire." I looked in the car and sure enough, there was a camp saw, a hatchet, and a bunch of fire starters. We learned to make those in Girl Scouts when I was in junior high. They were just sawdust and paraffin, poured in a paper muffin cup. I started breaking up the smaller bits of the limb and sawing off bigger chunks as Misty rummaged around in the trunk to see what else we might have.

"The packs have clothes in them."

"Huh. I was kind of getting used to the gown."

"Isn't it scratchy?"

"I think it was when I put it on this afternoon. Maybe I've just sweated and wiggled enough that it softened up. It actually feels kind of comfortable now. More like a bathrobe."

Before long, I had a fire going and Misty was heating water for instant hot cocoa. Roadkill had finished his kibble, done his business, and settled down on my feet.

It had been my own sense of rebellion that inspired me to wear my boots under my gown. And nothing else but underwear.

We hummed happily and sipped our cocoa, watching the campground darken outside the range of our firelight.

"UH... EXCUSE ME... Pardon me... Not to intrude, but would you kind people have a cup of that you could spare?" a voice asked out of the darkness. I was startled. Misty was startled. Roadkill was asleep. Good guard dog. Not.

A kind of scarecrow-looking guy was standing at the edge of our campsite, looking longingly at our cocoa. By scarecrow, I don't mean tall and skinny. That's me, remember? I mean he had kind of ragged clothes on, a straw hat, and an old flannel shirt that looked like he'd slept in it under a pile of dead pine needles. He had kind of straw-colored hair sticking out under the hat in all directions. He was leaning on a walking stick almost as tall as he was and had a backpack on. Misty recovered first.

"Got a cup in your kit?" she asked. "We can spare a packet of cocoa and hot water."

He swung the pack off his back and detached a tin cup from the side of it. This he handed to Misty and then dragged his pack closer to the fire so he could sit on it. Misty prepared his cocoa and handed it to him, then picked up her own cup and started to sip.

"Thank you. Thank you kindly. Travelers need to help each other out," he said. I listened carefully. His voice sounded more cultured than he looked.

"We have absolutely no idea what we're doing out here," I blurted out. "Nice to have company."

"I haven't much, but I've a little prime ganja I'd be willing to share." He rummaged around in a side pocket of his pack and pulled out a baggy and a pack of papers. Misty and I just looked at each other with big eyes and grinned. A little weed would make our impromptu cam-pout a lot more pleasant.

Now, it's not like we're big potheads. I mean that, really. That doesn't mean we've never toked up a bit, though. It's never really a bad thing, and a guy who's high on weed is usually too mellow to be a threat. I didn't see where he pulled his lighter from and didn't see him put it away. He took a big drag and held the pinch out to me. I sucked in a bit and held it, passing the blunt on to Misty. She always gets to coughing on her first hit, but she sucked a second in and managed to hold that. She held it back out to Scarecrow, but he already had another in his hand and was lighting it up, so she handed it back to me. She had that same look of almost instant change of space I knew I got when I smoked. I sucked in another lungful of the potent weed.

"This is good shit," I said, using as little of my stored breath as possible. He waved his arms around a little and ended up pointing downriver.

"Got it down that way," he said. "Traded some work for it."

"What kind of work do you do?" I asked, weaving a little. I expected him to have been planting crops or something. Misty held up a burning twig and I lit the blunt again.

"Oh, you know. 'Bout the same as you, I 'spect. I fix stuff for people. Broken things, mostly," he said.

"Like... uh... teapots?" Misty asked. I looked at her trying to figure out where that example had come from.

"I guess I could glue one together. Mostly, I fix people," he answered. I nodded knowingly.

"Like setting bones?" I asked, remembering there just happened to be a doctor in the diner who looked like most everyone else. I took another hit. I was not high enough to understand what he was saying yet. Misty took it from me and had a nice long drag.

"Oh, no. You know. Like broken relationships, broken promises, broken homes. Basically, just try to fix broken people." I needed another toke before I let that truly sink in. He must be like a psychiatrist or something.

"That seems like a noble calling," I said, thinking about the fact that all I'd done since graduation was drive and kill a robber. "I seem to specialize more in breaking things."

"No," he drawled. We were all dragging out our words a bit. The smell of weed hung around us like the smoke from the campfire. "Well, maybe you break the peace now and then, but I can't see you breaking anything valuable. We might fix different kinds of things, but I'd say you're a Fixer, too."

"Tell me more about that, please," I said. I was fascinated by listening to him talk and found I didn't want him to get up and leave just yet.

"That noble dog you have at your feet," he said. "I'd say he was broken and alone when he found you. You gave him hope, friendship, food, and love. You gave him the ability to rise above his lowly station to become your faithful companion."

"Not much of a guard dog," I chuckled. "Let you walk right up to our fire."

"He knew I was no threat. You see, here's the thing. There are people in this world who are out of whack. They become obsessed with their own villainy. Some of them go so far as to deny the humanity of everyone but themselves. I can't do anything about a person like that. He's not just broken, he's shattered. But you... You can give him peaceful rest. Take away his burdens and stop his madness. It's your way of fixing things."

"Kill 'em. I'm not sure I like that." I hadn't thought a whole lot about what motivated that nameless guy in the diner. Was he just a man who was broken beyond repair and I sent him on to his permanent rest? I didn't want to dwell on that. It was killing the high.

"Well, a warrior needs to be prepared to go to war when the cause is just," Scarecrow said. "You'll find strange things that people need to be protected against. Things those people can't protect themselves from. You'll rise to the occasion and find a way. You, Miss Warrior Wizard, are the hope for hundreds of people you'll meet on your journey. You're a different kind of fixer than I am, but you fix things I can't." He stood and rinsed his cup under the pump.

"What do I do?" Misty giggled. Yeah, she giggles a lot when she gets high.

"Oh, that's easy. You fix her," he said. "And a fine cup of cocoa. Thank you kindly for that. It will keep me warm all night. May the road rise up to meet you and may you have a gentle breeze at your back. Something like that." He shouldered his backpack and pulled a couple more blunts out of what looked like thin air and handed them to me. "You might need more later. Journey on." He thumped away with his walking stick and disappeared into the night.

"WHAT DO YOU think that was all about?" I whispered. Misty moved her stool over closer to mine and leaned against me. She held the last of the first roll against my lips and managed to not burn me when she held the flame to it. I sucked the hot smoke into my lungs and she dropped the remains before it burned her fingers. We just sat there while the fire crackled and enjoyed the high, looking up into a star-filled sky.

"There's so many stories in the stars," she sighed. "Heroes and legends and tall tales. We just met one of them and he got us high and left us dry. I'm just a speck among the stars sent here to be your fixer." She started giggling again and I joined her. We scuffed out the fire and poured another pot of water on the coals, then crawled into our tent. She'd arranged everything inside the tent with our packs on either side of the door, a place for us to put our shoes, and our sleeping bags laying open with one on top of the other.

"We sleeping in the same bedroll?" I asked stupidly.

"Somebody's got to keep me warm." She pulled her clothes off and crawled under the covers. Roadkill came in and lay down across the entrance to the tent. I zipped it up in case there were bugs flying around in the night. I slipped off the gown and the stupid mortarboard. Set my boots aside and crawled in with her. She was right. The body heat with both of us under the cover was pleasant and we'd be asleep before long. I went over all the strange events of the day. I thought it was going to be a normal high school graduation day. Instead, I heard a mysterious voice while the stadium seemed frozen in place, I was given my grandfather's prize '68 Fairlane, my aunt hopped in the car with me and my dog, and we took off on a road trip following an antique map that suddenly appeared in my diploma folder. Then we stopped a robbery, I killed a man with my mortarboard, we found a campsite where none had been marked on the map before, and a strange scarecrow of a man sits down with us and shares a smoke. And weird stories I was sure I was supposed to understand more of than I did.

"I don't think we're in Kansas anymore," I whispered.

"Hon, we were never in Kansas," Misty giggled. "But I think you're right. I think the minute we got in that car, we went off to a different world," she said. It was my turn to giggle.

"You been reading that Hobbit stuff again? Or Harry Potter? Maybe we should light another joint."

"I'm bein' straight forward honest about this as I see it," she insisted. "Pop gives you a car he's had for fifty-three years. Just hands you the keys and says, 'Bye-bye.' We take off and you've got a TripTik in your diploma folder—no diploma, I noticed. Every time we want something, it's suddenly marked on the TripTik where we should get it."

"Yeah. I see where you're going with this," I said. "We stop at a diner and everything looks normal except they let Roadkill in and feed him right alongside of us. Then a guy tries to rob the place and shoots the cashier, so I kill him with my cap. And everyone acts like that's all normal. They give me his wallet and gun. A doctor happens to be there and says the cashier will be fine. A sexy waitress cleans the blood off my mortarboard, which shows no sign of having been used to kill someone, and puts it back on my head. Then they give us our meal for free, including packing us a to go bag for breakfast. We just walk out and get in our car and everybody waves like we're some kind of heroes."

"You. Like you are the hero, my sweet niece. But listen. It gets better. Just when we decide we need to stop someplace for the night, the TripTik points us to this campsite that's marked with your varsity letter. Then we discover the car is packed with everything we need to make camp."

"Oh, wait. Wait. You forgot the part about me getting scared half out of my wits by a snake in the toilet."

"It was in the toilet? I thought…"

"Okay. I imagined it was in the toilet. It was really in front of the door," I sighed. "And then we sit down for a nice cup of cocoa in front of our little fire when a fixer-upper shows up. He trades a cup of chocolate for a couple of MaryJanes. And tells me I'm a fixer, too, but some other kind." I yawned, certain I was about to drift off to sleep, but we had something important we were supposed to get to. "It's all a bunch of strange stuff that combined to make a strange day. But nothing that couldn't possibly be explained away with a little logic and reasoning. Like the robber might have just been scared when I threw my hat at him and they tossed him in a dumpster to teach him a lesson. And that we just missed a turn-off into town at the bridge that was lit because we were too obsessed with scaring ourselves with stories of trolls. It's all simple stuff. There's no otherworld stuff going on."

"Do you know how many coincidences have to be stacked up on top of each other to equal the load of bullshit you just dished out?" Misty asked. "You read that philosophy book in school, just like I did. The simplest answer, no matter how improbable, is usually the right one. It happened when we got in the car and started it up. We were moved into an alternate universe in which all these things make sense. Put an arm around me. I'm still cold."

I wrapped an arm over her and we stopped talking. The thing about weed, though, is that after the initial high and talking and everything, I end up lying there waiting for it to be over. Like, okay, I've had enough of this now. I'm ready to not be high anymore. Okay?

Misty was asleep a long time before me as I kept going over and over all the things that happened and tried not to agree with her conclusion. I failed as I finally fell asleep.

Chapter 3

Thunder Mountain

WHEN WE FINALLY crawled out of our sleeping bag in the morning, it was only because Roadkill was whining at the tent flap and I was afraid he'd claw at it. I looked out and couldn't see anyone else in the campground, so I stepped out of the tent and stretched, trying to get rid of the weed hangover. What a weird night! Well, all day, really. I grabbed what was left of the tinder and wood I cut up the night before and started up a fire. I figured since we had a coffeepot there must be coffee in the supplies somewhere. As soon as the wood was lit and burning, I pulled on my gown, grabbed my towel, and headed for the washroom. Dumb of me to go barefoot, but I didn't trip on anything or step on any broken glass, so I figured it was okay. I did look around the entire latrine and shower area, though, carefully checking to be sure there were no creepy crawlies hanging around.

I started the shower running and it actually felt good and hot and washed away a lot of my pot hangover. I lathered my hair and washed my body, never even wondering where the shampoo had come from. It just felt good to rinse the sweat and smoke off me and feel like a human being again.

I looked critically at my sports bra and court pants and they seemed clean enough. Maybe my standards were failing me. I put 'em on and then donned my robe again, tying it shut like a bathrobe with the light blue cord instead of zipping it up. Outside, Roadkill startled me, prowling around. I caught myself before I screamed. The good dog was just doing his job, protecting me. I rubbed his ears and we headed back to campsite 33.

As soon as I got back, Misty brushed past me on her way to the washroom. "Watch the coffeepot," she instructed. "It should perk about five minutes, I think. If it's too weak or too strong, we'll know to change things next time." She had her skirt and shirt on and grabbed her towel. I nodded to Roadkill and he followed her down the path, watching out for her while she showered. Good dog. I started packing up the tent after I got my boots on again. I got everything folded and ready to stow, but I decided to wait for Misty to load it. She's a genius at packing stuff up. And I did manage to get the coffeepot off the flames somewhere around five minutes later. Maybe ten. I'm not sure. I poured a cup of it.

"Hey, this coffee isn't bad," I said as Misty and Roadkill came back to camp. "Let me get you a cup."

"Oh, yeah," she said taking her first sip. "That'll do nicely. Hey! The diner packed us breakfast. The bag's in the front seat."

"That's too bad. We probably should have put it in the cooler. I forgot all about it."

Misty retrieved the bag and looked into it suspiciously. She pulled out a paper carryout container and gently opened it, as if something might pop out of it. Then she sniffed and grinned at me. She handed me the box and pulled the second one out of the bag.

I looked in the box she handed me and found a hot, steaming breakfast of biscuits, sausage, eggs, and gravy. I mean it was steaming like they just took it off the grill. She had one just like it. There was even a box in the bag for Roadkill, too. Misty handed me a fork and grinned at me.

"Don't say it," I commanded. "I don't believe in magic. It must be some new kind of food container that holds the heat. Mmm. Dang, this is yummy." The food tasted like it just came off the grill.

"Uh-huh," Misty said.

"Okay!" I yelled to the campground. "I admit I'm not sane and am experiencing a lucid dream or a drug-induced hallucination or something." I turned to Misty who was still smirking at me. "It's either that or admit we're in a different reality than the one I knew. Whichever, I'm just glad you're here with me."

"Oh? You aren't going to confess to kidnapping me from my planet and making me your helpless slave?" she asked, blinking her eyelids at me innocently.

"Well, that's appealing, too. Just make up whatever wild-ass story you want and I'll agree to it. Nothing makes sense anymore." I gulped down more of the coffee and wondered at how good it was. "The question is, why are we here?"

"Oh, that's easy. To fight for truth, justice, and the American way." I guess the way she was standing with her carry-out box in one hand and her fork raised like a torch was supposed to be some heroic pose.

"This is the voyage of the Fairlane 500. Its five-year mission: To explore strange new worlds; to seek out new life and new civilizations; to boldly go where no teenage Warrior Wizard has gone before!" I declared.

"Let the adventure commence. The road beckons. The journey is ahead," Misty joined.

"The journey of a thousand miles begins with a single step," I answered as we packed our belongings.

"One ring to rule them all!" Misty declared. I looked at her and snorted.

"To infinity and beyond!" I said, starting the car. I checked the back seat to be sure Roadkill had made it into the car. He was already asleep. "Where to, Miss GPS?" I asked. She scrambled to get the TripTik out and locate our campsite.

"It says that way, along the river road. Looks like it could be a long trip."

MILE 188

IT WAS AROUND an hour later that we were nearly shaken off the road by a crack of thunder. It was so loud and shook the car so much that I pulled over and got out to look at the tires, thinking I'd blown one. It was quickly obvious that a storm was coming in like nothing I'd ever seen before. I jumped back in the car.

"We need to find shelter!" I yelled as I put the car in gear. Misty scrambled to open the TripTik and pointed ahead.

"On the right just ahead."

I tried to figure out where she was pointing. The only thing I could see was an old barn off the road a ways. Then I saw the sign that said 'Treaty Shelter,' and pointed right at the barn.

"That's it?" I said. I pulled into a dirt lane that I was sure would be running with mud. When we reached the open barn door, I turned around and backed in. I wasn't going to risk needing to turn around in order to get out. We got hit with a few huge drops of rain as we pulled in. I shut down and leaned my head back against the headrest and closed my eyes a second. "Sure hope this is safer than being out there," I sighed. I felt things getting darker and opened my eyes to see the barn doors closing. A guy wearing buckskins was pushing from one side. I jumped out of the car and shouted. "Hey!" Roadkill was out beside me in an instant. "You're shutting us in!"

"Don't want the doors open while the storm is out there," a guy on the other side of me said. I jumped and turned to see a grizzled old farmer with a straw hat and bib overalls pushing the other side door closed. In a second, the last of the outside light disappeared. Misty popped out of the passenger side of the car.

"Is it safe?" she called. Not that I could be in time to save her if it wasn't. I needed to talk to her about not taking such huge risks. The farmer went back to the side of the door and fiddled with some panel until a few lights came on in the barn. That made me feel a little better. Until I looked around.

The barn was huge inside. I didn't think it was anywhere near that big from the outside. And it was full. I don't mean full of people, though there were quite a few. The barn was full of animals. They each kept to their own little space, but none seemed upset by the others. For example, there were a dozen or more rabbits off to the right and three foxes curled up asleep about eight feet away. I did a quick inventory and saw deer, wolves, rabbits, foxes, mice, badgers, elk, wild cats, and a black bear, as well as a dozen of what I had to assume were people, though a bit shorter than average. I'm tall, but these were shorter than Misty by a good bit. I thought at first, they must be children.

"This is a treaty shelter," the man in buckskins said to Misty. Tall, tan, and good looking. And, of course, drawn to Misty like a fly to shit. "Everyone is safe here during the waking of Thunder Mountain."

"Thunder Mountain?" I said to the old farmer next to me. "Isn't that a train ride at Disney?"

"Can't rightly say," the old man answered. "Folks here call it that because of the storms that come up all of a sudden. Getting caught out in one could kill you. That's why we have treaty shelters like this one. Everybody's safe and harmless while they're in the shelter."

"Wow!" Roadkill was sniffing around, but seemed to understand that there was no prey here for him. A rabbit was standing on its hind legs as if it were talking to him.

"Watch out over there, though," the farmer pointed toward a dark corner where shapes were moving on the floor. "We don't usually allow their kind around here, but once they're inside, we have to abide by the rules. Just never sure if they will. Snakes don't live by the same rules as other creatures."

"Jackie, this is Hunter," Misty said as she dragged the handsome guy in buckskins over to us. "Hunter, this is Jackie. She's the reason we're here." Got thrown under the bus with that one, didn't I? I realized I didn't know the farmer's name.

"Mister? I'm Jackie," I said turning toward him.

"Honor to meetcha," he said. "I'm Amos McCoy. I'm kind of the head of this clan." He waved over to where the other people were gathered, settling in as if they planned on a long stay. They even had a couple of tents they set up at one side of the barn. I almost started humming the theme song for an old TV comedy.

> *Grandpappy Amos, the head of the clan—*
> *Roars like a lion but he's gentle as a lamb...*

"Well, we'll be outta your hair as soon as the storm passes over," I said.

"Might as well settle in. Soonest will be early tomorrow morning. Could be two or three days by the time waters recede enough to drive out."

"Two or three days?" I exclaimed.

"You got somewhere we need to be, Hon?" Misty asked. She was still looking longingly toward Hunter, who had gone to join yet another group I hadn't noticed. The more I looked around, the more I saw in the dim light. Deer fawns and wolf pups lay down together with a cougar cub. It was downright biblical. In the back of the barn, domestic animals gathered—pigs, cows, sheep, chickens, horses. I was sure I saw a few llamas. The barn seemed to go on forever.

"We have a common fire pit for the humans and animals that prefer it or need it to cook," Amos said. "You're welcome to pitch a tent nearby."

We opened the back of the Fairlane and pulled out camping gear to set up at the back of the car.

"Do we even have food?" I asked my aunt.

"We've never opened the cooler," Misty said. "Might be a good time to look before we have to go back and throw ourselves on the mercy of Hunter's clan."

"What, not Amos?" I snickered.

"Look at him!" Misty said. "Have you ever seen a man more perfect?"

"No. If that's your cup of tea, have at it," I said, shaking my head. I really couldn't blame Misty for the instant infatuation. He was handsome. He just looked like too much work to me. We repositioned things and opened the cooler—and stood staring at it.

"I'd say we're in good shape for a couple of days, at least," Misty squeaked. "It looks like Mam unloaded her entire freezer into the cooler, including all the prepared casseroles she put up." We pulled one out of the cooler that looked like it would feed the two of us. Hopefully, it would thaw before time to cook. We'd figure out a way to heat it when it was closer to dinner. We set up the tent and threw our bedrolls in it with our packs and then unfolded our campstools to sit and wait out the storm. There was plenty more thunder that rattled the old barn and a few children huddled closer to their mothers—both human and wildlife. Misty set a pot of coffee on the fire and we waited for the smell of fresh coffee to tell us it was ready. Then we just sat there staring around us at what it must have been like on Noah's Ark. Heck, maybe we *were* on Noah's Ark and when we come to rest after the storms it will be against some mountain in a foreign land.

As we were sitting there, a golden red spotted tabby cat jumped up in Misty's lap, eliciting a little gasp as it's needle-like claws got purchase on her bare legs. Roadkill raised his nose to sniff at the little bugger and then went back to lying on my feet. I could hear the rumble of the cat's purr as Misty stroked it.

A little kid approached us and just stared intently at my graduation regalia. I reckoned I should probably put regular clothes on, but this was like running around in my bathrobe and was really comfy. He pointed at the varsity letter.

"Were you in a lot of battles?" he asked. A couple more kids got up close to listen.

"Well, if you mean contests or games, yeah, I guess so. There's twenty to twenty-five in a season and I played four seasons. These little patches underneath are for the seasons I played in that sport. Four basketballs," I said pointing at the flaming emblems. "Four track seasons." The patches were a pair of track shoes with wings. "Three softball." I pointed to the bats with a ball flying off the end. "And four volleyball." The volleyball coach had no imagination and the emblems were just of balls. I couldn't point out any official school emblems for my participation in disk golf. And I could only play intramural soccer because it conflicted with volleyball.

The kids sat down at my feet and absently started scratching Roadkill's ears. I guessed they wanted to know more. The first kid affirmed that.

"Did you slay any giants?" he asked.

"Well, now that you mention it... I'm a pretty big girl myself. There aren't that many that stand above me. But we played the Cornwall Giants in the last contest of the tournament this year, there was a girl who stood over seven feet tall. And just a freshman. That poor girl probably never will get a date," I said. The kids just gasped at the description. "It was the last few seconds of the game and we led by just a point. It was a hard-fought battle. They got the ball to their giant under the net and I thought it was all over. But I gave it everything I had and when she went for the layup, I jumped and smashed the ball right back in her face. I felt kind of bad about breaking her nose and she bled all over, but we won the game and I got the trophy."

"Wow!" the kids all said.

"I want to be a Warrior Wizard," the little boy said.

"Study hard in school, eat your vegetables, and grow up strong," I said. "I'm sure you can become anything you want to be."

After a couple more stories, the kids wandered off playing some complicated game where there were good guys and bad guys who had a big battle. As far as I could tell there were no rules but they had to freeze like a statue if they were tagged unless one of their team-mates tagged them back to life. Several animals ran and jumped around with them.

I looked over at Misty and I guess she found the one thing in the treaty shelter that could get her mind off Hunter. The cat was purring up a storm and Misty was sound asleep where she sat.

WE JOINED SEVERAL other women and a couple of men at the campfire when it looked like folks were getting ready to cook dinner. We tossed our lasagna in a frying pan and let it heat as the others chatted and prepared food. When all the food was ready, Misty and I started to dip a scoop of lasagna onto our plates and it was quickly followed by all the others plopping a scoop of whatever they'd made onto our plates. We responded by putting a spoonful of lasagna onto any plate that was held out. By some miracle, the last plate held out got the last scoop.

We'd stumbled onto a potluck dinner and I was happy for all the food we'd been given, though I couldn't iden-tify what some of it was. I fed some scraps to Roadkill to supplement his kibble. I saw Misty feeding the cat from her plate. She'd also managed to get Hunter seated next to her and with him sitting cross-legged on the dirt floor and her on her campstool, it almost looked like he was her pet as well. I half expected her to feed him scraps off her plate. I chuckled, wondering when Misty would ask if she could keep him. I resigned myself to sleeping alone for the night.

One of the women in Hunter's tribe had a guitar and played some old folksongs that everyone could sing along with. Then I got the surprise of my life when she broke out into "The Ballad of the Warrior Wizard," which she apparently made up most of as she went. But there was a chorus that everyone seemed to know and joined in on, much to my embarrassment.

Horns sound her coming, blare her name
"Make way the Warrior! Cheer!"
Drums beat a rhythm, let villains beware
The Warrior Wizard is here!

WHEN I WAS ready to crawl into our tent for the night, I found Misty in her nightshirt in the tent. She was attacking her hair with a brush as if it deserved to be punished for something.

"You okay, sweetie?" I asked.

"Grr. That no good handsome hunk of a cheater," she growled. "He's married! He took me back to his tent and nicely invited me in to meet his wife. And they expected me to stay with them!"

"Well, that sounds like it has possibilities," I laughed.

"Not for me! I'm not into any polygamous marriages or to being a mistress or a concubine or whatever they call these things out here in Neverland. Sorry, but you're stuck with me."

I couldn't help myself. I rushed to her and wrapped

her in my arms, giving her a big squeeze. She cleared her throat and I let her go kind of quick like.

"I'm just glad you're still with me," I said. "I was afraid it was going to be just me and Roadkill moving on."

"I wouldn't have abandoned you," Misty sighed. "It was just a fantasy."

We crawled into our bedroll. Roadkill took up his position across the entrance and I started to zip up the tent. A golden red spotted ball of fluff came bounding through the opening just before it closed, stepping on Roadkill's nose. He had a little bark, but settled back down to sleep. I slid into the bedroll to find a cat taking up space between Misty and me. She was petting it and it was purring up as much thunder as there had been outside. I chuckled and went to sleep.

THAT WAS SHORT-LIVED. I don't think I'd been asleep an hour when I heard a woman yelling, "Lukey! Lukey! Where did Little Luke go off to? Grandpappy! Luke is gone. Where is he?" There was genuine panic in her voice as I could well imagine there might be. The barn was full of wild animals, including a corner full of snakes. Not to mention the wolves, bear, and wild cats. I unzipped the tent and stepped out with Roadkill when Misty caught my ankle.

"Here! You better put this on," she said, handing me my robe. Well, dang! I'd stepped out of the tent in my underwear. I grabbed the robe and pulled it on, wrapping the light blue cord around my waist. I needn't have worried since most of the people gathering around were just coming from bed in various stages of undress.

"Now when did Little Luke go missing?" Amos demanded.

"I was just checking on all the children," the woman said. "He wasn't in his bedroll and I checked all the others. We have to search everywhere!"

"Well, we know he's safe here in the treaty shelter."

"But there are animals…"

"The treaty has never been broken," Amos insisted.

"He isn't in the barn," a small and frightened voice said. We all turned to the little girl who grabbed onto what I assumed was her mother's nightgown.

"What is it, Hassie? Where is Luke?"

"He made me promise not to tell."

"Mothers override promises," the woman said. "If you know where Luke has gone, you need to tell us right away. He could be in danger."

"He said he was going to slay the thunder monster and become a Warrior Wizard," the little girl said.

"How did he get out?"

"Through the slat in the toilet stall."

I'd been back to the toilet stall. It was really nothing but a hole in the floor that you squat over. It also let more of the rain in than the rest of the barn, which kept the floor washed down. We all headed back there to take a look. Indeed, there was a loose board that could possibly let a person through. But certainly not the hunk that was Hunter. He tried, but the rest of the boards were secure.

"We'll have to go out the big doors," I said.

"Can't," Amos declared. "When the doors are opened the treaty comes to an end. The animals can't go out in this weather."

"I'll be right back," I said. I ran to the car and grabbed the big flashlight from under the seat. I pulled my boots on and tied them quickly. When I turned to head back, Misty slammed my stupid mortarboard onto my head.

"Take the hatchet, too. You never know what you might meet out there."

"Thanks, hon," I said; accepting the hatchet I shoved it through my rope belt.

"Come back to me," she answered.

I ran back to the stall and people stood around waiting while I wiggled my way between the boards. Don't know if it was good I was so skinny or bad.

The wind and rain were fierce. I turned on the high beam of the LED flashlight and started to flash it around. Which way would a small boy go when he was faced with this kind of rain and wind? He said he was going to slay the thunder monster. This was Thunder Mountain. He'd head uphill.

I turned my face into the rain and took a few steps, nearly blown back to the barn. A little kid like that could have been blown to kingdom come in this gale. I kept scanning the area with my light as I fought my way uphill. There was a muddy area that I slipped on and saw a small shoe stuck in the mud. I was on the right track.

I wondered what Little Luke had taken as a weapon to slay the monster. He was maybe five or six years old. What would he even have?

I didn't have to wonder long. I caught a glint of steel in my light and focused on it. As I came nearer, I saw that Lukey had armed himself at the cookfire. He had an aluminum pot on his head and a small iron skillet in his hand. He was backed up against a tree and as I approached nearer, I saw he was intent on something in the grass. I looked where he was looking and there was a small army of snakes slithering toward him.

Damn! It! I hate snakes in the best of weather. In this weather, with them closing in on a frightened boy, I really despised them. I scanned the ground to make sure there were none in my path to reach him and approached from just behind. I was just in time to see a dark snake rise up from the grass and strike at the boy. I didn't have time to think. I just grabbed one of the cords from around my neck and snapped it at the snake like a bullwhip. By some miracle, the snake strike hit the iron skillet Luke was holding. It stunned it just long enough for my cord to wrap its neck and snap it. The crack was echoed by distant thunder.

If you've ever wondered, by the way, the crack of a whip is caused by the loop traveling along the whip gaining speed until it breaks the speed of sound and creates a sonic boom. At that speed, even a light braided cord will do serious damage to a snake. It writhed on the ground, but without a head, the death throes were brief. The other snakes turned toward me and I cracked the cord again. They dropped to the ground and slithered away in the rain.

I tossed the cord around my neck and grabbed Luke. I don't know what inspired me, but I bent and picked up the headless carcass. We headed downhill, retracing as well as I could, the path I'd taken from the barn. We even stopped to grab his missing shoe.

Squeezing in through the gap in the boards was harder than getting out because we were both soaked to the bone. Inside there was a lot of screaming and dancing around. I just stumbled to the fire and tried to get warm.

Chapter 4

Puss 'n' Og

I WAS ALMOST too exhausted to care when I finally huddled over the fire. Suddenly, Misty was there beside me, scrubbing at my hair with a towel while she simultaneously managed to get my cap and gown off. Might have had help with that. I don't know. I took the towel and kept drying myself as she removed my boots, sports bra, and court pants. I was about to complain when a blanket was wrapped around me and I sat shivering on a campstool. I saw that Luke was undergoing much the same treatment across the fire from me. I spotted Hunter and called him to me.

"Hunter, show me how to skin and eat a snake," I said. He grinned at me and quickly produced a knife to slit the skin and strip it from the carcass. Then he opened the carcass and pulled out the guts and organs, which he immediately threw on the fire. Shortly, the meat was cut into sections and placed on skewers to roast. I wasn't sure, but maybe I could do that in a pinch. I grabbed my own camp knife and scraped the inside of the skin clean. Hunter got the idea of what I was doing pretty quickly and brought a bucket filled with some kind of alcohol solution by the smell of it. He trimmed off the rattles and handed them to me, then rolled the skin loosely and submerged it in the solution. He sealed it up and set it aside.

I gave the rattles to Misty to store away for me. Didn't know what I'd do with them, but I had a notion they'd be important someday.

By this time, Luke had been chastised and then encouraged to tell the tale of his adventure.

"I tracked the monster up the mountain to its lair," he said brazenly. "But the monster has many heads and it surrounded me. The chief head of the monster looked me in the eye and said, 'I will make my dinner of this fine strong boy.' But when he struck, I battled him and hit him in the head with my iron hand. The monster drew back again, but just then the Warrior Wizard appeared with fire in her hand that blinded us all. She threw a lightning bolt at the monster that severed its head and the crack of thunder was echoed deep in the mountain where the monster lives. The rest of its many heads pulled back into the cave and disappeared like a turtle in its shell. Then the Warrior Wizard and I took our trophy of the monster's neck and came back to the shelter. But even now, you can hear the monster moaning in his cave as the rain dies outside."

That Little Luke was quite the story teller. We all took a bite of the snake meat from the skewers, dipped in some kind of spicy sauce Amos produced. I was impressed by Luke's story, but the guitar player struck up another rendition of the Ballad of the Warrior Wizard with new words commemorating the battle against the Monster at Thunder Mountain. Everyone sang the chorus again.

"Thank you, Warrior Wizard, for coming to the aid of my brave son," his mother said. "One day may he follow in your footsteps."

"The skin of the monster's neck being tanned by Hunter shall be a belt for Luke, the youngest Warrior Wizard. Wear it with pride. Um... And may the Force be with you," I finished lamely.

My clothes were hanging on a couple of the cooking tripods next to the fire, so I crept back to my tent. Misty got me into the blankets and that damn little cat lay on one side of me while Roadkill pressed against the other. Misty zipped up the tent and crawled in next to the cat. It was only a few minutes before I was sound asleep.

THE MORNING DAWNED clear and bright, but true to Amos's prediction, the lane leading to the treaty shelter was mud that could eat my car. I collected my underwear from the drying rack, embarrassed that everyone had seen my bra and drawers hanging there. It looked like someone had washed it all and even cleaned the mud from my gown. It was dry, so I just pulled it on and tied it shut. I noticed that Luke's mother had taken it upon herself to clean the bloody end of my white cord. It looked good as new.

We impatiently waited out another day in the barn. Most of the wild animals took off as soon as the doors were open. A few were in small pockets alone, watching people and other animals. I noticed there were no longer any snakes in the corner of the barn. Good. Anyplace I saw them now, I could just kill them. We had another communal dinner and Hunter awarded the snakeskin to Luke with instructions on how to wash it and let it dry. That was one happy and proud kid. That night we were serenaded by the guitar player and I swear she'd added in another bunch of verses to the Ballad. I'm sure I blushed crimson.

"WELL, MISTY, WHAT do you think. Should we break camp and leave?" I asked as I sipped my morning coffee and looked out at the dry lane back to the road.

"I suppose. There's nothing to hold us here," she said, glancing back toward where Hunter's tribe was getting ready to move on. We packed up the tent, bedroll, pots and pans and the coffeepot. Amazingly, Misty managed to pack everything back in the hatch of the Fairlane like it had never been disturbed.

The folks left in the shelter showered us with praise and a few gifts. We were given fresh eggs and a slab of bacon. That would be nice in the morning. At the last minute, Luke came running up to me and gave me a big hug.

"I'll be brave, just like you," he declared.

"Being brave is not enough, young warrior," I said. I tried to sound old and wise, but don't think I was succeeding. "Grow strong. Run lots. Practice with your weapons, and play ball." He looked at me as if I'd said something profound.

"Here, Warrior Wizard. This is a gift from my family to yours."

"Jerky?" I asked looking in the sack.

"Your new companion will need meat. This will last until she is old enough to hunt," he said. New com... what? I looked in the car and next to Roadkill in the back seat was a spotted cat, curled up under his chin.

"Misty?" I called.

"She wants to come with us. And Roadkill approves. It's so nice to have a little kitty with us," my aunt whined.

"You know that isn't a housecat, don't you? She's

going to be as big as Roadkill in a few months," I said. Misty's face fell.

"You mean she's a..." she looked to her side and a large cat, about knee-high, was bumping against her leg. Misty scratched the cat between the ears and I could hear the purr all the way on the other side of the car. "...bobcat?"

"Yeah. She's going to be as big as her mother there."

"Well, she'll really keep us warm at night," Misty said brightly. She bowed to the mother and said, "We'll take good care of your little girl. Don't worry about a thing." The bobcat turned and stalked off with two more cubs following her.

I turned the key in the ignition and the 390 rumbled to life. Just putting my hands on the steering wheel made me feel powerful. We waved to our new friends and pulled out of the barn onto the lane and eventually to the highway.

"Which way?" I asked.

"Right," Misty responded, looking at the TripTik. I turned onto the highway and we continued on our adventure.

MILE 261

"WELL, ARE YOU convinced yet?" Misty asked. "You went out and slew the Monster of Thunder Mountain, saved a kid, told tales of derring-do, and had an entire ballad sung about you. And as we were leaving, Mr. McCoy was painting your Warrior Wizard symbol on the side of the barn. That should be enough evidence for even a skeptic like you."

"You know that was a snake I brought in," I said. "The fire in my hand was a flashlight. The lightning bolt was me cracking a cord like a whip. Lukey's iron hand was a frying pan."

"And the bobcat in the back seat?" Misty persisted.

"You would bring something along as a reminder," I sighed. "What are you naming her?"

"Well, we got her on the side of a mountain. But I don't want to call her Thunder. Though her purr rumbles as loud as this car. I was thinking maybe naming her Shasta. That's a good northwestern name for a mountain cat," Misty said.

"Mmm. Isn't that the name of that creme soda that's so good?"

"Now that you mention it... Maybe we could find some next time we stop."

"Speaking of stopping, my gas gauge still says full. We'd better find someplace to check the tank and make sure we've got fuel. Anything on the map?" I asked.

"Now that you mention it, there's a town ahead where we have to cross the river again."

"I was beginning to think this world didn't have towns."

"See? You do believe!"

"Fine. Is there a gas station in said town?" I demanded. I hadn't really seen a town since before the mountain pass yesterday. That was before we really began the adventure part of our road trip. I wondered if that was where we made the transition. Drive up the pass in one world and down in a different one. I shook my head. That's ridiculous!

"Franklin's Everything Store and Gas Stop," Misty said. "It should be on the left. Look. over there."

I drove on up to gas station/convenience store/hardware/coffee stand and pulled in. Misty handed me my wallet. "You'll need a card, Warrior Wizard." *Bitch.*

"Why don't you go in and see if they have decent espresso," I said. "I'll fill the tank and come join you. They must have a restroom, too."

She went into the store which looked like it filled all the business needs for anything people in the town wanted. I put my gas card in the pump and started to fill it up. The hose clicked off as soon as I squeezed the lever. I tried again. Nothing. I looked at the pump to be sure it was running. It reset with my card and was still displaying all zeroes. I checked to see if there was another button I had to press to select the grade or something, but it only had one grade of gas. I clicked the handle a few more times.

"They don't like you to top off. Spills poisons on the ground," a voice near me said. I jumped and turned to see a coverall-clad dude wiping his hands on a dirty rag walking over. I looked up at his face and corrected my opinion. Seemed it was a female grease monkey who was talking to me. The name patch on the pocket declared her name was Dale.

"I just pulled up and can't get it to start pumping," I said. She reached past me and squeezed the lever, causing it to click again. She handed me the hose and pulled a metal stick out of her belt that looked a lot longer than she was. She fed the stick into the tank, pinched her fingers at the point where it met the lip, and pulled it out again. Six inches below her fingers, the stick was wet with gas. She wiped the stick with her rag and slid it back in her waist, taking the hose from me and hanging it up.

"Aye-up. You're full up," she said. She took a walk around the car, inspecting it and looking under it. She looked through the windows and was surprised to see the dog and bobcat. She popped the hood and just looked while she was still holding it up with her hand. She whistled. Finally, she dropped the hood and turned to me. "Yep. Got yourself a good one here. I haven't seen one of these in years and years." She didn't look to me to be any older than I was. Years and years? "This baby will go a long way on a tank of gas."

"Really? How far?"

"Long long way. Miles and miles."

"You're telling me this car won't run out of gas?" I said.

"You're the Warrior Wizard," she said. "You ought to know."

"Yeah, well, I haven't really gotten used to that," I mumbled. Okay, I had a full tank of gas that didn't go down. And a cute girl mechanic. And Misty was in the store.

"Thanks for the info," I said. "Can I buy you an espresso, Dale?"

"Mmm. Guess we can see if the machine is working again. Goes on the fritz as often as a McDonald's ice cream machine." She laughed as if that was the funniest joke ever. I'd seen the meme.

Inside, the old guy at the cash register just looked at us and gestured toward the other side of the store. I took the long way getting there as Dale went to check on the espresso. I figured I'd run into Misty here somewhere. Interesting stuff in this store. I decided I'd pick up a few additional supplies. Bag of cat food to supplement the jerky and a couple pet dishes. I glanced out the window at the car. We'd left the doors open and Shasta and Roadkill were just stretching beside the car. I wasn't worried about them. I figured if they wanted to ride with us, they'd be in the car when we were.

I found the Shasta Creme Soda and collected a couple bags of chips. I dumped that stuff on the counter and went back to exploring. In the next aisle, I picked up window cleaner so we could clean the glass in the car. I wanted to find a car wash or at least a hose to rinse the mud off it. Pop would throw a fit if he saw it like this, so I picked up a jar of carnauba wax, too. I saw a campy pair of fuzzy dice I decided to hang from the mirror. I saw some lawn and garden stuff and grabbed a machete. That would have been better for fighting the snakes than my hatchet. I never even got that out of my belt. I definitely needed more rope and picked up a spool of it in the hardware area. There was a slingshot and box of shot in the sporting goods that I decided might come in handy since I didn't want to go shooting the gun in the glove box or even showing it around. The shot was clay balls that would melt into the earth with the first rain.

I took it all up to the counter and headed toward where the grease monkey had disappeared. When I rounded the end of the shelf full of insect repellent, I saw Misty behind the espresso counter, tinkering with the machine. Dale crawled out from under the counter, where she'd apparently been helping. In a minute Misty twisted something in place and turned a dial. Steam came out of a nozzle. She shut it off and looked up as she was tamping down grounds in the basket.

"Latte, ladies?" she grinned. I just nodded and she set to work steaming milk. "The vacuum breaker valve was stuck. Little wash and air running through it and it's good as new. I knew all that time working as a barista at Starbucks would come in handy one day." In a couple of minutes, we all three had lattes and she'd pulled a straight espresso to take to the guy at the counter. He sampled it and started nodding.

"Interest you in a job? Folks will start coming in soon now the machine is working," he said.

"Oh, we're just passing through," Misty said.

"I can make the shots when people start coming, Pap," Dale said. She scrubbed at her hands with some grease remover and zipped out of her coveralls. She had a cute little uniform under them. It was a short skirt above a very nice pair of legs. The tube top was only a band a couple inches wide. "They tip really big when I'm not in my coveralls," she grinned. Hell, I was going to tip big, too.

"Goodness, you've been shopping," Misty said. "Look at all this stuff!"

"Just figured we should get some supplies. You didn't think about food for your cat, I noticed."

"I knew you'd think of everything," she grinned.

As soon as Dale was behind the bar, people started coming into the store. Some shopped around a bit, some seemed to know what they wanted and went straight to it. All of them came to the counter with a latte in hand and paid the old man.

"Is there a carwash around here?" I asked the old guy, gesturing back toward the door.

"The kids wash the cars," he said. "Keeps 'em out of trouble. I gave 'em your wax and window cleaner already."

I looked outside and half a dozen kids were climbing all around the car. They had a hose and were lathering it up good. I wanted to run right out and protect my car, but Misty laid a restraining hand on my arm.

"Looks like they know what they're doing, hon. Might as well let them keep doing it," she said. I watched, but was nudged by a furry head. I looked down and Roadkill and Shasta had apparently wandered in with the people coming into the store. "We need treats!" Misty said, rushing off down and aisle of pet supplies. The old guy behind the counter leaned across and offered the two animals treats from a jar next to the register.

"We get their kind in here quite a lot," he said. Misty returned with two boxes of cat and dog treats and paid for them. I thanked the proprietor and we picked up our double armload of purchases and headed for the door.

What a weird place.

We were just at the door when it flew open and a mountain of a man came through, knocking us on our asses. "Coffee!" he bellowed.

People started scattering as he moved toward the coffee bar. Roadkill growled and Shasta hissed at the indignity heaped upon us. While Roadkill sniffed up Misty and me to be sure we were okay, Shasta bounded after the giant and leapt to the counter in front of him.

"We got problems," I said. It looked like that guy could smash little Shasta into the ground with one hand, even while he was grabbing hold of Dale and shoving her toward the machine with the other. I jumped up and snatched the gold cord off my neck. I caught up with the dude as he was attempting to sweep Shasta off the counter. He brought both massive hands around to grab her and I cracked the cord like I had at the snake. It wrapped itself around his wrists and tied them together. I gave a jerk on the cord and he spun to face me, still looking in disbelief at his bound hands.

"You need to learn some manners, buster," I shouted. It might have been the first time he'd been addressed by someone tall enough to look him in the eye.

"Uhhhhh..." Not very eloquent, but the breath he exhaled...

"God! And get a toothbrush! Have you ever heard of a bath? Who are you anyway?"

"Og," he stuttered, still disbelieving that he was tied up and seemed unable to move.

"Og? As in Ogre?" I demanded. Shasta paced up and down the counter with her fur standing on end, hissing.

"Ogden," he whispered. Misty brought a package of mints and threw one in his mouth.

"Ogden, why do you think you can just barge into a respectable business and knock people over while you shove your way to the front of the line and demand service? Tell me that!" I shouted.

"Um... Big," he said.

"Well, not big enough, are you? You come with me. You can't have coffee until you're civilized." I just turned and dragged him out of the store toward my car. The kids were working hard at the polish and the car gleamed. "Hey, kids. This dude needs a shower. It's gonna take all your scrubbing power," I said.

That was all it took. The kids understood at once, and Og just stood there with a look of horror on his face as they attacked with hoses, brushes, and soap. I kept a firm grip on the rope just in case he decided to try to get away, but once they started, he just stood there submissively, letting them scrub him down.

Sadly, Og's clothes were in such filthy tattered shape that they mostly disintegrated and fell off. What was revealed was quite a specimen. He was about six-six and barrel-chested. He had a lot of hair on his body and a bit of a belly on him, but you could just see the muscles bulging from his legs and arms.

Dale suddenly appeared in her coveralls with a ladder and a toothbrush. She started scrubbing at his mouth and then made him rinse with a cinnamon flavored mouthwash. She proceeded to comb and cut his unruly hair, showing quite a barbering talent. She even produced shaving cream and a razor to clean up his face. By that time, the kids had worked their way down to his bare feet and a statuesque hunk of a man stood in front of us.

Dale disappeared and was back in a few seconds, in her barista outfit and holding an extra-large latte. She looked at me and at the rope as the kids finished toweling him off. Someone showed up with a clean coverall that looked like it might even fit him.

"Can I trust you to behave like a civilized human being instead of an ogre?" I demanded. He worked his jaw a couple of times, like he wasn't used to speaking much.

"I behave," he finally said. "Sorry for fuss."

I flipped the cord and it unwrapped from his wrists. I watched him closely as he put his arms through the sleeves of the coveralls. I wondered how they happened to have a pair big enough to fit him.

"Now, Ogden, that isn't so bad, is it?" Dale said, moving up to him. She offered him the coffee cup and he took it gratefully, even managing to say, 'thank you.' "You see, all I ever wanted for you was to be a little civilized. You can still run the mountains and hunt and fish. And I know you like the cars. I'll teach you all about how to fix them and we'll find you one of your very own. How's that sound?"

"Good," he grunted. "Real good." He held the coffee cup up to salute her.

"Then at night, instead of hiding out under the bridge, you can come to my place. I got a big soft bed, just right for the two of us. You'd like that wouldn't you?"

"Good, Dale," he said. Wow! He was getting more than one word at a time out.

"Thank you, Warrior Wizard," Dale said, looking at me. "I been trying to tame this big galoot for nigh on two years now. He just gets excited when I turn the coffee light on." She pointed at the store and a neon sign was lit that just said 'Coffee.'

"You think you can handle him now?" I asked.

"Oh, Ogden and me are going to be just fine, aren't we big guy?"

"I like Dale. I be good for Dale."

There was a yowl from near his feet. Shasta was standing in front of him, hair still standing on end. She snarled. Ogden got down on his knees.

"Nice kitty," Og said. "Ogden not hurt kitty. Ogden sorry. Nice kitty." He held out his hand and I half expected Shasta to take a bite out of it. Instead, her hair started to lay back down and she rubbed up against the offered hand. Little slut. He scratched her ears and the purring commenced.

I looked around at the people watching the little display of affection, the kids who had washed the car, the grinning proprietor of the store.

"Well, I wish you folks well," I said. "Guess it's time for us to finish packing our supplies and hit the road. Who knows what tomorrow may bring?"

People brought our things to us and Misty packed them in the back of the Fairlane just as if there'd been room for everything. Shasta and Roadkill jumped in the back seat and I turned the ignition. The big engine came to life and rumbled as we waved and pulled out of the convenience store gas station.

"Where to?" I said.

"That way," Misty said pointing toward the bridge. I'd swear that was the same bridge we crossed a few days ago—streetlights and all. Oh, well. The road still lay ahead.

Chapter 5

Four Stars

"JACKIE THE OGRE-TAMER," Misty laughed. "Scrub him down, kids!"

"All right already! I was scared out of my mind. A guy as big and strong as him? He could have just snapped the cord I wrapped around his wrists. It was just taking him so much by surprise that made it succeed. Nice touch throwing a mint in his mouth, by the way."

"Did you see the way he looked at Dale?"

"Or the way she looked at him? It was like she was just waiting to get hold of him and give him a shave and haircut."

"Nice job of it, too. I can just hear them now as they plan to name their first baby Jackie," Misty said. "I saw the way you looked at him when he was all cleaned up. Worried for a minute that I'd have to go on the rest of this quest by myself."

"Oh, please. I mean he was quite a handful when he was all cleaned up, but that's not what I'm on the hunt for," I said.

"Exactly what are you on the hunt for?"

"Good question. I didn't know I was on the hunt for anything when we started out the other day. Now it seems like there should be some meaning to all this."

"All what, dear niece?" Misty asked sweetly. I frowned at her.

"Okay. Let's suppose for argument's sake that we are in a separate reality. That someplace after graduation, we magically transported somewhere and I'm a Warrior Wizard and you are still my pain in the ass but much beloved aunt," I suggested. She wrinkled her nose right back at me.

"We are," she declared flatly.

"Then why? Why send a six-foot-three beanstalk off into a different dimension dressed in her graduation gown and army boots, with her dog and her aunt and a hot car that never runs out of gas? What I'm saying is that if... IF, I say... if this is a different dimension, there must be some reason I was chosen to enter it. And that reason has be more than stopping a robbery, killing a snake, and taming an ogre. I might believe all this is some supernatural shit, IF and WHEN you can tell me what the purpose is," I said. I was sure I had her here. She was quiet for a minute. The silence was deafening. Only I couldn't tell if the rumble I heard was the engine or that cat being bathed by my dog. That's not evidence of the supernatural, is it?

"Okay, I'll play this silly game of speculating with you. There has to be a higher purpose to your calling. However, there is a lower purpose, too. You have to learn to accept yourself for what you are, and learn to flourish. And you do that by constantly having your character tested and overcoming whatever dangerous situation lies before you. You find strength of character to act and stop a robbery. You find the courage to go out alone in a deluge to rescue a little boy from snakes. You take one look at a huge man raising Cain and see beyond the exterior to tame him and make him a part of society. Those are all things that reveal your character and show what kind of person you genuinely are."

I thought about what she was saying while I sang along with k.d. lang on the radio.

> *gonna walk away from trouble with my head held high,*
> *then look closely, you'll see luck in my eyes.*

I looked over at Misty and she was singing along, too. She was also fiddling with something in her lap and I realized she was sewing something.

"What you got there, girl?" I asked.

"Little project I picked up back at the store while you were taming the ogre," she said. "You got them snake rattles and no place to put them. Too bad we couldn't have pulled its fangs. Anyway, I just thought I'd sew up a little bag to put your trophies in."

"Don't plan to pick up a lot of trophies, but having the rattles someplace safe would be good."

"Now, you don't get to escape the question so easy. That's the part of the quest that's about you. But there's lots of ways to show what a person is made of that don't involve getting transplanted into another dimension. There's something about *you* that is needed in this world. The place hasn't looked that broken and in need of fixing like Scarecrow said he does. I don't see armies gathered on the horizon getting ready to wipe out the innocent people we've met. But there's a quest here and it seems like you probably know what it is or you wouldn't be here."

"Well, the next thing is to pull into that roadside so the kids can stretch their legs and pee. Me, too," I said.

"Yeah. Me, too," Misty sighed. I'd avoided the question again.

It was just a little roadside park, but it had restrooms and a pump for water. We gave the pets a bowl and each had a Shasta Creme Soda and munched from a bag of chips while the two explored around the park and Shasta practiced her pouncing skills on an unamused Roadkill. He came up to me with the cat on his back and whined.

"What a good boy you are," I comforted as Misty picked up Shasta. I petted Roadkill and made sweet over him. "Okay, kids. Don't know where we're going, but we should head out." They scampered into the car and settled in with Shasta giving Roadkill's ears a good cleaning. I could just hear him moaning, 'This is so undignified.' We pulled back on the highway.

MILE 394

WE BEGAN SEEING small towns more frequently. I guess that didn't take much since we'd seen only one small town in the past 250 miles or more. At one we stopped for a potty break and bought ice cream at a little stand. Nothing happened. It was a relief. I was beginning to think that every time we saw people, I'd need to do something heroic. It was nice to not even be looked at twice.

"So, quests generally divide up into three categories," Misty said. She was not letting go of this whole quest thing. "You could be here to kill or destroy something. That's the classic Tolkien. Take the one ring to Mount Doom and cast it into the volcano. Lewis: destroy the snow queen and liberate Narnia. Second, the find or recover quest. Indiana Jones and the *Raiders of the*

Lost Ark. Brooks, *The Sword of Shannara*, once again to destroy the Warlock Lord and free the four lands. Finally, the rescue quest. Rescue and resuscitate Snow White, free and resuscitate Sleeping Beauty, find the white tower and rescue Rapunzel. Classic fairy tale scenarios.”

“Those last ones are all damsel in distress scenarios,” I sighed. “Just not interested in rescuing and resuscitating a princess from the dragon.”

“Ah, but the thing is, you might be called to do any of them in the process of fulfilling the main quest. You can’t just look at a robbery in progress and say, ‘Not my circus, not my monkeys.’ You have to take action or you aren’t the hero of the story.”

“I had to go rescue the little boy because I’m the hero,” I said, mulling over the words. “I had to tame the ogre or I wouldn’t be a hero. Are we sure being a hero is what I’m meant to be? Maybe you’re the hero and I’m the trusty but completely inept driver who is constantly getting in trouble. That would work, wouldn’t it?”

“Ha! Who in their right mind would cast me as the hero? I’m only here to be with and support you. And try not to be the one who needs rescuing.”

“Still, all that gives us is the directive to keep being heroic, even though I have no idea what it’s all about.” We drove on a mile or two and started to see signs of a major settlement. Billboards advertising hotels, restaurants, insurance companies, and DUI lawyers. “I’m tired and hungry. I say we get a room at that nice hotel. I’ll treat you to a decent meal and a clean bed with a hot shower.”

Misty opened the TripTik and scanned the page to see where we were.

“Might not want to do that,” she said. “The TripTik says ‘don’t stop here.’ We should go on a ways.”

"I said I'm tired and hungry," I snapped. "I'm not waiting for a stupid map to tell me where to sleep for the night." I pulled into the hotel entry way and a valet ran out to take the car. I held up my hand to stop him when he came to the window. "Just tell me where to park that's safe. I don't give the keys to this baby away to anyone."

"I'll personally guarantee the safety of your vehicle, ma'am," he said. "I'm a trained professional driver."

"I'm sure you will guarantee the safety of my vehicle and I'll tip you well to do so. But you need to point me to a safe parking space."

He started to speak again but stopped when he actually looked into the car and saw me. I swear, he jumped back five feet and snapped to attention.

"Yes, ma'am," he said. "We'll watch your vehicle carefully. Just pull into that center spot over there." He pointed and I drove to the designated space. There was an empty space on either side of me and when I got out of the car, I saw the valet running to place yellow cones blocking off the other two parking spaces. He ran back to his station by the door and I saw him on the phone. I was surprised no bellman came out to carry our luggage, but I guess after the way I treated the valet, it was understandable.

The animals got out of the car with us and we picked up their dishes, our backpacks, and the bags of animal food. People stood aside as we made our way to the registration desk. Apparently, the valet had already reported our arrival. Misty handed her credit card to the desk clerk and he looked surprised. He ran it and handed us key cards.

"Top floor. Executive suite. It's the best we have. Room service is waiting to attend you," he said. Then he jumped back and left the desk. Neither of us had signed anything. There was no one else there to ask a question of. We went to the elevator and pushed the button for the top floor. It was eerily silent. The executive suite was lavish.

"Woah! Is this the life?" I asked, tossing myself onto the huge bed. What luxury! Misty kept prowling around. "Hey! Lighten up. They're giving us the royal treatment. Doesn't that compute in your book of heroes?"

"Jackie, haven't you noticed how weird everyone is? Yes, they're giving us the best of everything, but they're all running from us like scared rabbits. Everyplace else we've been might not have been wealthy, but they were friendly. This all makes me nervous," Misty said.

"Oh, come on, Auntie. Let's go down to the restaurant and have a big dinner. Steak tonight. I saw the sign in the lobby pointing to the steakhouse. Bet they have the best you've ever tasted."

"I don't know, Jackie..." She was still stumbling around the room, so I grabbed her hand and opened the door. The animals jumped out of the room and scanned the hallway like they were bodyguards. I just headed to the elevator and tapped the lobby floor.

Apparently, our appearance in the lobby again was unexpected. There were several people milling about talking, but as soon as we were noticed, a hush fell across the room. Everyone moved away as we made our way to the steakhouse. No one met us at the reception desk, so we just walked in and sat at a table where we thought we'd be out of the way.

"We don't serve your kind in here," a burly man in a dark suit said, approaching our table.

"They're service animals," I explained. "And they've already eaten."

"I was talking about you," he said glaring at me. "You'll have to leave."

I was pissed, but whatever they thought 'my kind' was, I wasn't going to get violent. I stood and turned to Misty.

"Come on, Misty. We'll get room service like you said," I said. The animals got up to follow me.

"I said you had to leave. Not her. She can stay. In fact, I insist she stays," the man said. I was beginning to suspect he wasn't the maître d'. Misty started to stand and he shoved her back into her seat. I stepped forward to move him away and three more guys suddenly appeared, bearing down on us. Roadkill growled and jumped one of the guys, knocking him to the floor. Shasta leapt to the table and scratched the hand that was gripping Misty, then bit it when he swung at her.

I swept my mortar board off my head and pointed it at the assailant coming from our right. He closed so fast that his eye ran right into the point of the cap and he fell back, clutching his face. The fourth guy held up his hands and backed away. I pulled Misty behind me and began backing toward the door. I whistled and the animals immediately left their prey and joined us in our retreat, growling and hissing all the way out the door. We returned to the elevator and went to our room.

"OKAY, I ADMIT it was a bad idea to stop here," I said when we were safely back in the executive suite on the top floor. "Let's pack up and leave. There must be someplace in this town where we can get a decent meal and a bed for the night." Misty kindly didn't say 'I told you so.' She went to collect her pack and the pet bowls. Roadkill nudged at my pack and I bent to pick it up. He just kept bumping his nose against a side pocket. I opened it up and found his ball. When I pulled it out, he was all happy and bouncing around waiting for me to throw it for him. Pets can turn on the protective growls one moment and the playful whine the next.

I bounced the ball and he leapt to grab it, proudly showing his prize to Shasta as I picked up the pet food and we left the room. Roadkill held his ball as we left, as if it was a trophy of his victory. The lobby was empty as we left. This place must be haunted or something.

The adventure wasn't over, though. The first thing I noticed when we walked out the door was that the valet was lying against his stand, tied hand and foot. He was struggling against a gag and I reached down to remove it.

"I tried to protect your car, but they're after it. They hit me and tied me up," the valet cried. I dropped the bags of kibble as Misty started working on the ropes tying the valet. I stepped off the steps of the hotel to look where I'd parked my car. Three guys were looking it over. One had a sledgehammer in his hands and seemed to be preparing to break and enter.

"Step away from the car," I barked in my best imitation of a Batman voice. The hoods looked up. The guy with the hammer looked at me and sneered.

"Or what, Warrior Wizard. Gonna sic your kitten on us. We're ready for you," the dude said, showing his leather gloves. They were all wearing goggles, apparently prepared against getting stabbed in the eye, too. Roadkill nudged at my hand and I found his wet slimy ball there. The sneering dude raised the sledgehammer and I threw the ball at him.

I played softball in school, just like all the other sports. I could pitch, but I played first base because I could stretch halfway to second without taking my foot off the bag. And I had more 3-6 and 3-6-3 double plays than any first baseman in the state. When I say I threw the ball at him, I mean I pegged it with all the fury I had when throwing first to third.

It was a good throw. Hit him right in the forehead. Sounded like the crack of a baseball bat. As he started to crumple, there was a second crack. The ball had ricocheted off his forehead and hit the guy next to him with just as much force. Roadkill the wonder dog had jumped forward and caught the ball as it bounced off guy two. Double play. Two outs with one throw. The third guy adopted the familiar pose that I'd seen in the steakhouse. He threw up his hands and backed away until he could turn tail and run.

I shoved the two unconscious bodies out of my way and opened the hatch. I'd no more than tossed my pack in when Misty and the valet arrived with the rest of our gear. They shoved it in the car while I opened the door for Roadkill and Shasta to jump in. I turned to the valet and handed him a wad of cash from the diner robber's wallet.

"Thanks for watching the car," I said. Misty and I piled into the car and laid rubber getting out of there.

MILE 404

"DON'T SAY ANYTHING about it," I commanded my aunt. "Just look at the damn map and find out where we're supposed to stop for the night."

"Night's Inn on the far side of town," she said. Somehow, we made every traffic light through town and I was careful not to speed or even change lanes without a signal. Still, I didn't see any patrol cars as we proceeded through town.

Night's Inn proved to be a run-down no-tell motel. It was actually Knight's Inn, but the 'K' on the sign was burned out. I went into the office to register. It smelled of disinfectant soap, but I guessed that meant it was clean. An old guy in a backwards baseball cap looked up from behind the desk.

"Well, you're finally here," he said peevishly. "You were expected two days ago."

"Two days ago, we were holed up in a treaty shelter waiting out a torrential storm," I said. "Who are you that you'd be expecting us anyway? Just give us a room and point us to a restaurant where we can eat without getting attacked again."

"Us? Attacked? Oh, no. What have you done? This was supposed to be a simple pass-through. Haven't you read your instructions?" he demanded, handing me a huge door key chained to a plastic paddle with the number 105 engraved on it. Looked like it had once been painted but the paint had worn off so just the engraving was left.

"What instructions? If you have something to do with all the weird stuff that's been happening to us, I'd like a clear explanation." I was leaning over the counter where I was towering over him.

"You were given a packet of travel documents when you received your weapons. Did you not read it?"

"My diploma folder? My weapons? Oh, yeah. Misty pulled the TripTik out of it and we've been following along. This is now Mile 404." Misty and the animals came in and wanted to know what was taking so long. The old guy was apoplectic.

"But this is all wrong," he said. "You were supposed to be alone. And you have familiars, too? Very bad. I need to check with my superiors."

"Well, while you're checking, I want food. Where can we eat?"

"Over there," he waved generally toward an equally shabby restaurant on the other side of the parking lot. "I know none of this looks ritzy and elegant like that hellhole on the other side of town, but we're safe. Just be thankful you didn't stop there."

"We did," I said.

"Oh, no. Bad. Very bad. Go! Go eat and take your travel documents with you. Read them! Why do you think we go to all the work of preparing things for a hero? And then you don't bother to even read the instructions! Go! Get food. Everything has been upset. Go."

Okay. We were going. We stopped at the car long enough to grab my diploma folder. Misty had crammed it under the front seat after she pulled the TripTik out. We entered the restaurant a little warily, but nothing seemed all that out of place. We were greeted and seated by a nice little old lady who used a lot of little endearments and touches as she got us settled and bent to welcome the animals. They both seemed to be happy to see her and settled right down at our feet. Misty slipped treats to both of them. It all reminded me uncomfortably of that diner we went to the first day out. I kept scanning the room for potential robbers. The other diners, however, seemed scarcely to notice us.

We hadn't even looked at menus yet when a waitress hustled to our table with a tray full of salad and coffee. It was a big bowl of salad that we served ourselves from. Of course, the waitress gave us the first serving. She reminded me of the waitress at that diner, too. Nice butt.

"I'll have..." I started.

"It'll be right up," she answered. "If there's anything else I can get you, just yell 'Suzy!' and I'll be right here." She hustled away from the table, pausing to grab a coffee pot from the serving station and refill cups as she went through the restaurant.

"Did we order?" I asked.

"Hon, things have gotten too weird for even me to comprehend. And I'm the queen of weird. I thought we were just on some simple quest. What was the motel clerk guy upset about?" Misty asked.

"Apparently, there was more stuff in the diploma folder than just the map. Did you see anything?" I reached for the folder.

"Oh, yeah. There's a bunch of papers in there. Looked like a passport, too. I didn't figure we'd need that right away, anyway. I didn't really look at the other stuff after I found the TripTik." She handed it to me.

"Supposedly, there's a bunch of instructions in there," I said, opening the folder. *Geez!* The thing was packed with maps, tickets, instructions on recharging the car, how to use the mortarboard, cords, and stole, and a sheet called 'Instructions for the Warrior Wizard.' How could my aunt not have thought any of that was important? I broke the seal on the instruction sheet and spread it out.

"Oh, this is exciting," Misty said. We were both shoveling down the salad so fast we hardly noticed when Suzy approached the table again. I looked up as she set a huge porterhouse steak sizzling on a metal platter in front of me. She gave Misty some kind of fancy chicken breast with vegetables and a sauce that looked like it was the antidote for a diet. Our coffee cups were refilled and

Suzy smiled sweetly before she drifted off to tend to other customers.

"Did we order?" I asked again. I cut into the steak and it nearly fell apart. Perfect! Charred on the outside and barely warm and red on the inside. The instructions would have to wait a few minutes while I gobbled down the steak and loaded baked potato that was on the platter next to it. The thing was huge. I estimated it might be two full pounds of melt-in-your-mouth heaven. Misty attacked the chicken with moans that were decidedly sexual.

When we'd finished the main course, Roadkill was crunching up the big bone out of the steak and Shasta was delicately tearing apart pieces of the chicken from Misty's plate.

"Oh, man! I couldn't eat another bite!" Misty moaned. Just then, Suzy appeared again to whisk away our dirty dishes and return with two huge hot brownies with ice cream and chocolate fudge syrup. And more coffee. Somehow, we managed to devour them!

"I really need to read these instructions now," I said. "All I want to do is crawl in bed and sleep after that meal, but the old man seemed to think this stuff is urgent." I unfolded the instruction document and flattened it on the table so we could read.

> *Dear Warrior Wizard,*
>
> *We are in desperate need of your help. The most precious jewel of our crown has been stolen and we fear may never be seen again without the assistance of a powerful Warrior Wizard.*
>
> *Please follow the directions on the map and drive to East Love as quickly as you safely can.*

*Make only one overnight stop and make haste
to our fortress. DO NOT become involved in local
affairs or have any more congress with people
you chance to meet than absolutely necessary.*
 *The future of our domain lies in your hands.
You are our only hope, WW.*
 Regis Ferdinand Rex

Well, shit, Obi-Wan.

Chapter 6

A Pocketful of Beans

WE GOT BACK to our hotel room and spread all the documents out on the coffee table. I couldn't believe all we'd looked at was the TripTik. But, to be fair, I only told Misty to see where it said we should go. She grabbed the first thing with an answer. We never bothered to look further.

What we found was an array of miscellaneous information and travel documents. For example, there were a pair of "Bearer Passports" that said the bearer was permitted to cross from one land to another. I wondered what Homeland Security had to say about that. There was a charm that was the equivalent of a 'Get out of Jail Free' card. If you were imprisoned, it could be used to get you out.

The most interesting to me was the 'Weapons and Armor Manual.' It showed a picture of my entire graduation regalia, describing the use of each item. My mortarboard, for example, was the equivalent to Xena's Chakram. Well, I'd already discovered that. It could be used thrown or handheld. There was nothing about it returning to me, though. I guess that's what Roadkill was for.

The manual included a lot more stuff. Some that I had and some I'd acquired. The basketball in the back of the car could be used as a kind of Molotov cocktail, it burst into flames when throwing it. The hard ball I used to play catch with Roadkill was a kind of blunt projectile. The manual specified that a slingshot was an effective weapon against giants, but only if the giant was hit in the forehead. And my gown itself seemed to have some kind of protective powers, though I found the manual rather vague about that.

"Look at this," Misty said. She held out another booklet titled, 'The Book of Wizardry.' Hmm. I guess it made sense to have a separate book for the Warrior and the Wizard. Supposedly, I was both.

"Oh, crap!" I said as I opened it. "It's in French!" I need to tell you that I took three years of high school French as was required for graduation. French was the reason I didn't have a 4.0 grade-point average. I wouldn't have had a 3.5 if it weren't for all the AP classes I took. "I'll never understand the spells if I have to speak them in French!"

"Madam Auclair would be so disappointed in you," Misty said, citing our high school French teacher.

"Madam Auclair was *always* disappointed in me," I sighed. "I guess now, we just get some sleep until Regis Ferdinand Rex summons us or something." I hung my robe and regalia, with new respect for them. Then I went into the bathroom for a shower and washed out my underwear. It was surprisingly fresh yet. I wondered if there were a bunch of other spells on things that I didn't know about. Like the gas tank that was always full. When I came out of the bathroom, Misty threw a nightshirt at me and went to take her own shower. I was asleep before she finished.

I WOKE TO persistent knocking on the motel room door. I got up and automatically pulled my gown on as if it were a bathrobe, then went to see who was there. It was a little man. That's all I could describe him as. About three feet tall, it took a minute before his eyes had traveled all the way up to mine. He stepped back across the hall so he didn't have to crane his neck so far.

"The Honorable Warrior Wizard and her companions are invited to join Regis Ferdinand Rex for breakfast. Breakfast will be served in two hours. May I carry your response?"

"Um... We'll be happy to meet for breakfast, but you need to tell me where as well as when."

"Our sovereign prefers to breakfast at nine o'clock in the sun room of the fortress. I'll return to report your reply." With that he ran away from the door and jumped into a golf cart to zip away from the motel. I couldn't tell exactly where he was going. I returned to bed, but didn't bother to lie back down. I pulled out my backpack and rummaged around to see if there was anything appropriate to wear to breakfast with the Sovereign—whatever he was called.

"You should wear your official regalia," Misty said. "Apparently, cap and gown is the uniform of the Warrior Wizard."

"Why do I suddenly want to wear shorts and a tank top?" I asked. As I shoved acceptance of the idea that I was in an alternate dimension away from me, I realized I was becoming more and more petulant and whiny. I heaved a deep breath and pulled off the robe so I could put on my favorite sports bra and court shorts. I debated wearing shorts and a tank top under the gown, but I was really getting used to wearing it like a bathrobe and thought it rather funny that appearing before the Sovereign in my bathrobe and underwear was the height of politeness.

"You look very nice," Misty said. I sat at the desk in the room and she rubbed some kind of hair oil on my head and combed my short hair into place. She turned me toward her and applied a bit of foundation to my face and eyeliner. At least the lipstick didn't make my mouth look bigger than it already was. I looked in the mirror and decided I didn't look any worse than I had at graduation.

Misty got ready quickly by putting on lacy underwear and a cute sundress. Maybe it was a little short, but I was sure no Sovereign would complain about seeing Misty's legs. She had a pretty pair of high heel sandals. I, of course, wore wool socks and my army boots.

"Now all we need to do is find this place for breakfast." We took the travel documents all with us and seeing nothing around that looked like a fortress, got in the car. Both Roadkill and Shasta sat up in back, an unusual position for them.

"The TripTik says right and right again," Misty said, looking at our paper GPS. I drove out of the motel parking lot and turned right. Half a block farther on, I turned right again. "There should be a sign up here for Main Street. Follow it to the right again." We followed the sign and about half a mile later we saw it. "That's it," Misty sighed.

"Please tell me that isn't just the courthouse," I sighed. We'd made it to the town square and there was a huge castle-like structure in the middle of it. Stationed around the corners were the obligatory displays of cannons and cannonballs. Only these had real-life soldiers manning them, ready to fend off... something. What did the courthouse have to defend itself against?

We were waved into a driveway and up to a portico. I was shown a place to park and the four of us got out of the car. Doormen showed us the way and opened doors for us. I guess that's what doormen are supposed to do. There was no elevator in this old building. We were pointed to a vast sweeping staircase that split in the middle and led left and right. We followed to the right and then around a balcony to another staircase that was walled off from the main rotunda. At this level, a butler in formalwear met us and ushered us into the dining room where we were shown to the head of the table where a man stood to greet us.

He was absolutely ordinary in every way. He wore a dark suit and tie with a white shirt—all of which reminded me of the thugs the night before. He was a few inches shorter than me, but that was still an average height for men. He reached for my hand and I shook with him.

"Warrior Wizard and..." he turned to take Misty's hand "...consort. Welcome to the Sovereign Land of Victoriana."

"Your Sovereignty," we responded, nodding our heads forward. Misty had found that in a book of etiquette in our travel documents.

"And these, your familiars," the Sovereign said turning to Roadkill and Shasta. They both bowed. Apparently, their book of manners was more complete than mine. "How delightful. Please have a seat. Breakfast is the most important meal of the day, you know. And please, just call me Regis. No need to keep using titles while we break bread together."

"Likewise, Regis. I'm Jackie and this is Misty. Attending us are Roadkill and Shasta," I said as we were seated to the right of the man. Two women entered the room and took the seats to his left.

"Jackie and Misty, may I present my wife Regina Elizabeth Rex and daughter Princess Bridget Rex," Regis said. Somehow or other their first names all sounded like titles. They greeted us politely. I got the feeling the daughter was in her early to mid teens, though the mother didn't look more than twenty or twenty-five. Well, maybe a trophy wife. "We are so happy you could get here," Regis said as servants brought plates of food for us and set them on the table. I noticed they set plates that looked almost as appealing in front of the animals. And the food smelled delightful. It was just a good down home breakfast with bacon, sausage, eggs, potatoes, and hot black coffee. Everyone dug in.

"I understand there was a slight miscommunication and we were expected two days ago. I'm afraid our early instructions were lacking significant bits," I said.

"That happens when we're dealing with the other side. Had a minstrel come through once five years after she was expected. But it all balances out. We were expecting one person and received four," Regis said. "I am sorry to say, however, that the delay may have put the task out of reach."

"Your note said only that the jewel of your crown had been stolen. Must be pretty big. Diamond? Ruby? Emerald?" I asked. It would help to know what we were looking for.

"Oh! No! Language can be a great barrier to communication sometimes. It is our son who is missing," Regis said.

"And you've been waiting for me to get here to go after him?"

"Don't think so poorly of us," Regina said. "Regis sent an entire police company after them. We just knew a real Warrior Wizard would be better able to handle the situation. I'm afraid our police are not terribly efficient."

"Worse yet, I believe we may have been tricked into sending them. It has left the Land short of police to enforce the laws and certain criminal elements are taking advantage of the situation to gain a foothold in the city. Hopefully, you have not and never will meet any of the unsavory characters in that element," Regis said.

"We may have run across some of them last night when we got to town. We stopped at the big hotel on the west side of town for the night. We had to defend ourselves before we moved to the Knights' Inn," I confessed.

"Oh, dear. That's what Clark was going on about when he came last night. That means the Caesars have been warned that you are here. It could make it tricky getting you out of town to pursue the kidnappers. We'll set up a diversion when the time comes," Regis said.

"I'm afraid I don't understand the subtleties of what is going on," I said. "Perhaps if you could explain what has happened and what you want us to do about it, we could help you."

"Of course." Regis pushed his plate away and a servant swept in to collect all our dishes. Apparently, when the Sovereignty is finished, everyone is finished. "Eleven months ago, our son, Baron Federico Rex was in the park on the east side of the fortress. His governess was with him and the usual array of soldiers were patrolling the grounds. Suddenly, a fog arose, sending everyone into confusion. People were stumbling around, running into each other, and generally being worthless, amidst which confusion, the governess continually called out for her charge, all without answer. When the fog cleared, Baron was gone. Half a dozen soldiers were found slumped over the barrels of the cannons, and the governess was swinging on the swing set, singing 'Swing Low, Sweet Chariot,' which is all we've managed to get out of her ever since."

"Excuse me, Regis. This happened eleven months ago?" Misty asked. "And you were concerned about Jackie being two days late?"

"Why the sudden rush to recover your son?" I asked, following up on Misty's questions. "He's been gone nearly a year."

"We were certain we could recover him at first. Then there were negotiations that took forever. We finally realized they were simply trying to delay things until it was too late."

"Too late for what?" I asked.

"For the succession ritual next month. We hold a ritual each year in which the sovereign names his successor. Of course, that doesn't mean he's abdicating; only that a successor has been named. But once a successor has been named, which Baron was just before he was abducted, he must be affirmed on Succession Day each year. If he fails to appear, any other house in the Land could put forward their candidate for succession and call a vote. Old August is sure to put his grandson Valentine up for election. He would probably need only to intimidate a few extra people to show up and have the succession changed."

"It sounds like a bunch of internal politics and something I shouldn't get involved in. After this Valentine was elected as successor, your son, Baron, would be returned to you. It just means it would no longer be your line that succeeds to the sovereignty. Why would I care?"

"Valentine is both mean and incompetent," Regis fumed. "You're right. If he was a good person, I'd have no difficulty with surrendering the succession. But meanness and incompetence are a dangerous combination." He stopped and caught his breath for a moment. "And he would expect us to acknowledge the succession by marrying Princess off to him. If you bring back the jewel of our crown, I will betroth you to him and you will become the First Lady of Victoriana," he finally sighed.

Ish! I had no desire whatsoever to become betrothed to a boy I'd never met, who still needed a governess and was unable to defend himself. And across from me, I saw a person who agreed. Princess was seething. I shook my head.

"Where can I find this Valentine so I can make my own judgment?" I said.

"He hangs out at the resort hotel on the east edge of town. He usually has three henchmen nearby. He talks them into doing mean things, but when the tables turn against him, he proves himself a coward and runs away, letting the three take the blame," Regis said. "You really don't want to meet him."

"I think I might already have done so," I said. "Last night, we attempted to eat at the steakhouse there. Four men attempted to throw me out while keeping Misty with them. One of them is now missing an eye. The remaining three were around my car when I decided to leave, intending to smash it up with a sledge hammer. Two of them are probably recovering from headaches and minor concussions. I hope they're minor. In both instances, the last man raised his hands and ran away."

"That would be Valentine," Regis agreed. "Okay. If you don't want to be First Lady, I'll give you half of Victoriana. Not the best half, of course. The other half."

"I'll try to find your son and bring him back," I said. "No promises. I'm kind of new to this hero thing. I'll not do it for his hand or for half your kingdom. Not interested. That's so medieval. Come up with some other kind of reward when I succeed."

"Jackie the Beanstalk, Warrior Wizard, you shall have all the help I can give you," Regis said pompously. "I've already arranged for our armorer to go over your weapons and armor and make sure they are in good shape. The kitchen will supply any comestibles you need. If there is anything else we can do to help, please let us know."

The butler arrived and I was ushered out with Misty, Roadkill, and Shasta.

WE WERE NOT taken to my car, but wound our way down to the dungeons, if such a term applied here. They were actually below-ground offices and workrooms. There I met Tomas, the armorer. Looking at the walls of the armory was like looking at both a museum and state of the art weapons display.

"Ah, yes, yes," he said, holding up a sleeve of my graduation gown. "This is a lovely suit. Well-made. Protective. Nice color for you. Hmm. No pockets. We need to correct that. And this! Ah! You are tying your binding cord around your waist? The light blue should be hung from your neck with the white and gold. White for whip. Gold for submission. Blue to bind and hold." That sounded like a reasonable color to use for holding the robe closed, but he wasn't happy until he had it off and hung around my neck. That left the robe hanging open, of course. No big deal. I wasn't in dressy underwear. I was just wearing my workout things.

"Wow! You get right down to it, don't you?" Misty giggled. Tomas looked over at her.

"Really? You are going to battle at the Warrior Wizard's back dressed like that? Do you think this will be a stroll along the boardwalk on a Sunday afternoon? This will never do. Renée! Come out here and dress this companion appropriately. They may do battle in rugged terrain. We can't have her being torn to shreds. It would distract the Warrior Wizard." In a moment, a woman who was simply the female version of Tomas was examining and measuring Misty. She was thin and fussy, constantly batting Misty's hands away from where she wanted to measure.

"I suppose you have something for Shasta and Roadkill, too," I laughed. Tomas looked down at the two animals sitting at attention beside us.

"Oscar! Familiars to arm for battle!" he called out. The man who arrived could have been Tomas's twin. In fact, I suspected the three of them could be triplets. Oscar was down on the floor with the dog and bobcat, rolling around and talking to them as they played together.

"Oh, you are such brave and gallant and noble friends for the Warrior Wizard and her Maiden Companion. Shall we get you some armor to match theirs? You'll be the envy of all the other familiars. Come on. Let's get you outfitted." Oscar jumped up and ran out of the room with Roadkill and Shasta right behind him. I assumed I'd see them again eventually.

"Now, if we just had a good snakeskin for your belt, that would be what the well-dressed Warrior Wizard would wear," Tomas said, tugging the robe open and closed to see how much overlap there was.

"Sorry. Gave my snakeskin to a young would-be Warrior Wizard a couple of days ago. Good one, too. About six feet long."

"And you gave it to a child?" Tomas said in horror.

"Well, I still have the rattles."

"We will need them! Very well, off with it and let me get it fixed while we get you more armament." I pulled off the robe with all its regalia and handed it to him. He rushed out of the room with it while I stood in my Under Armour sports bra and court shorts. And my mortarboard. I had to laugh, just thinking about actually wearing Under Armour under my armor. I turned my attention to Misty. I think every part of her body that could be measured, had been measured. She was a little pink in the face. Renée stepped back and looked at her as well.

"Leather," she said. "The perfect companion piece."

"Really?" Misty asked. "Isn't leather awfully stiff and scratchy?"

"Ha! My leather will fit you like a second skin and feel better than the one you're wearing." She flew out of the room with Misty in tow, as fast as Tomas re-entered.

"Did you go get the rest of your weapons?" he demanded.

"I didn't realize I was supposed to."

"How else are we to equip you if we don't know what you have?" he said, throwing his hands up in the air.

"How do I get out of here?" I asked. Tomas slammed his hand down on a bell on the table and my escort from earlier popped into the room. He wasn't prepared to see me without my robe and looked startled.

"Take the Warrior Wizard to her car and help bring her weapons down here."

I followed the steward to the car with only a moderate amount of embarrassment. I grabbed everything I could think of that was in the book of weapons and picked up the pouch Misty had made with the rattles in it.

TOMAS MADE SURE the basketball, my mortarboard, Roadkill's ball, the slingshot and ammo, and the rattles were all to spec.

"You don't have any magic herbs or talismans," he complained.

"Why don't I just take one of those AR15s?" I said. He looked at me in horror.

"There is a reason those are locked up." He refused to answer any questions about the firearms and I was thankful that I'd 'forgotten' to bring the handgun in from the glovebox. He looked at the bag Misty had made and passed some kind of cloth over it, inside and out. He muttered that it would seal the leather so it would not leak the magic out. When he'd finished, he'd also revealed an intricate pattern on the leather. I wasn't sure that Misty was even aware the bag had a pattern on it. I hadn't seen it before.

He pulled a length of black cord out and laid it on the table.

"What's the special power of the black cord?" I asked.

"No special power. You use it as a garrote or to hang someone." He laid a handful of pebbles on the table that I thought might be more shot for the slingshot. On closer examination, though, they proved to be beans. "Magic beans," he said solemnly. I almost cracked up. Then there were a couple of easily recognizable weapons—a short sword and a knife. He pulled packages of herbs out of drawers, a feather, and a magnifying glass. I was wondering how I was supposed to carry all this stuff.

Misty reappeared, wearing a red leather bra top and skin tight pants. I whistled.

"Isn't this just the cutest?" she exclaimed. "Renée is a wizard with a needle. And look, it has pockets on the outside! Do I get any weapons?"

Tomas ran out of the room and brought back my robe and gear. He slipped it on my shoulder and if anything, it felt lighter and even more snuggly comfortable. Then he pulled the belt around me. The belt was silver that matched my stole. He showed me it had a lining where I could keep a little money. The sword and knife hung nicely from it, and there was a holster for the slingshot. Then he snatched my car keys out of my hand. Not having had anywhere to put them, I'd taken to wearing the keyring on my finger with the keys dangling off my hand. Tomas deposited the keys into my new pocket. There was a hook to hang the medicine bag from and he shoveled the beans into a pocket on the other side. Misty was given a nice knife and a staff that was almost as tall as she was. Her little high heeled sandals had been replaced with a pair of supple leather boots that matched her pants. Renée tied her hair back with a matching leather thong and after studying the whole effect for a moment pulled a large ruby from the desk and fixed it in Misty's exposed navel. I'm not sure how she attached it. It looked like it grew there. She nodded her approval and changed places with Tomas so they could each inspect the other's work.

That was when Oscar came back with Shasta and Roadkill. My dog was wearing a dark blue leather vest and a spiked collar! He came straight to me and sat waiting for me to inspect his armor and pet him. I did while Misty knelt beside Shasta and the bobcat jumped up on her bent knee. Misty automatically winced, expecting the bite of the cat's needle-like claws. She got a look of pleasant surprise on her face as the leather prevented the claws from penetrating. Shasta wore a red leather collar with a ruby hanging from it.

"The little one is growing fast," Oscar said. "She would outgrow a vest rapidly. However, these boots should expand as she grows." We looked and, indeed, Shasta was wearing a lovely pair of red leather boots on her hind feet.

"Aren't you just the most precious Puss in Boots there's ever been!" Misty exclaimed. "You'll be able to walk into anything with those mighty boots!"

We made sure we had collected everything we needed and came with. I bounced Roadkill's ball to him and he carried it proudly ahead of us as we finally left the fortress and made our way to the car.

As we were getting in, the short guy who brought our invitation to us in the morning, dashed up and handed me a packet of documents from the Sovereign. We resolved to actually look at and read this batch of papers before we left in the morning. We returned to the motel and went to dinner at the dumpy-looking restaurant across the parking lot.

Chapter 7

Guess Who's Coming to Dinner

DINNER WAS GOOD, but not nearly as extravagant as the night before. I had a nice stuffed porkchop with cornbread dressing, roasted vegetables, and rice pilaf. Yummy, but lots lighter than the two-pound porterhouse I had the night before. Misty had some kind of fish dish of unknown origin. She said she really needed to watch her weight if she wanted to keep fitting in the skin tight leather pants and bra top. I think the 'sexy quotient' of the outfit was much higher on her list of reasons to wear it than the fact it would protect her legs when we were in rough country.

After dinner, we sat at the table with coffee that Suzy kept filled while we went over all the documents included in the new packet. Mostly, these were documents legitimizing our quest. Assignment of temporary guardianship, for example. That way, if we were stopped after rescuing the kid, we had proof signed by the Sovereign that we were the proper caretakers. There was also a rolled map. Unlike the TripTik, however, this map had no roads or highways marked on it. It was a general map of the Land of Victoriana that showed the relative positions of major features, like half a dozen towns, a mountain range, a big river, a lake, and scribbled notes that were hard to read. After deciphering one of the notes, I wasn't sure I wanted to figure out the others. 'Here be the untamed land of man-eating giants.' I wondered exactly how old this map was.

The most useful note on the map, however, was one that circled 'The Dragon's Lair.' It said this was the last known location of young Baron Federico Rex. It looked like that was the direction we would be heading in the morning.

We finally left the restaurant, cheerfully waving and saying we'd see them in the morning. I was bushed. I got out of my robe and washed my undies before taking a shower and pulling on my nightshirt. Heaven knew when we'd be able to get another hot shower. I was asleep by the time Misty managed to wiggle out of her leathers.

THE KNOCK ON the motel room door heralded the arrival of the court's short messenger. He was not alone. I think he brought an entire kitchen with him. First, breakfast was served. Basic, but hearty—ham and eggs, dark toast, lots of coffee, and orange juice. They also had food to pack in our car. I opened it up and waited while they loaded more stuff in the back of the car than it could possibly hold. Misty and I left the car doors open so the animals could get themselves arranged when they'd done their morning business. They looked so sharp in their new clothes. I think Shasta was practicing walking on just her hind legs in her new boots. The spotted tabby actually looked quite dignified.

We looked at the map and compared it to the next batch of instructions on the TripTik. The cooks closed the hatch. The little messenger man saluted us, and spoke loudly so that all the four or five people within hearing distance could understand.

"The Sovereign of Victoriana prays good speed and a safe journey to Jackie, the Warrior Wizard and her companions. May you return to us with the jewel of our crown that the Sovereign Line of Rex may be continued and Victoriana may live in peace and glory." He saluted again and jumped in his golf cart. A panel van full of cooks followed out of the motel parking lot. He headed toward town and by the time he was a block away, the van lit up with fireworks shooting from its roof and a dark car pulled out to follow it. Oh, yes. A diversion.

"Mount up," I said. "It looks like the adventure has begun." There was a bark from the back seat. Misty bucked herself in and Shasta bounced into her lap. I turned the ignition and felt the big engine rumble to life. "Which direction, Misty?"

"Right, and straight ahead for a long way." The opposite direction of the fireworks. Of course.

"Here we go!" I admit to showing off a little when I peeled out of the parking lot.

MILE 499

"HOW CAN YOU possibly say none of this is real?" Misty complained. We'd been arguing all morning. She started it by stupidly asking if I believed now. I'd just as stupidly said, 'No!'

"It can't be real. It defies logic," I said.

"But you're still wearing your graduation gown and it has pockets! I've got a gorgeous new red leather suit on and a bobcat kitten sitting in my lap. We met the

Sovereign and have packed more stuff in the back of the car than there can possibly be space for. It has to be magic! We must be in a different dimension."

"No," I responded. "I must be dreaming. That's the only logical conclusion. I fell asleep—maybe during the commencement ceremony; it was boring enough. And I am sitting there happily dreaming along as if I'm in a LARP. And as for the robe, the pockets, the leather, the kitten—they are all evidence that I'm dreaming. Even the car. Pop would never give me his precious '68 Fairlane. And it was such a gas hog I couldn't have made it to the hardware store gas pumps on a single tank of gas. The bridges we've crossed have all been identical. Same type of construction, same streetlights—even in the wilderness. Like I'm projecting an archetype of my ideal bridge whenever there is one to cross. Towns come up when we want them to. Distances are meaningless."

"Then wake up!"

"No way! This is the most fun I've had sleeping since Dan Blackwell took my cherry. Just gonna sit back and enjoy the movie."

"Movie. That should be proof you aren't dreaming. Dreams are never linear. They jump all over, sometimes back to things that already happened. This is our seventh day out, and even the odometer is ticking out the miles consecutively."

"Speaking of which, I need to pee and the animals probably need a break, too."

"Roadside rest and viewpoint at the top of the pass," Misty said. "Just popped up on the TripTik."

"Next reason I believe it's a dream. Whenever we need something, that antique map suddenly has it marked on it." I pulled into the viewpoint rest area. It was pretty spectacular. "Now, I'm going to try to make it to the bath-room and back without waking up."

"Don't pee the bed," Misty snarked back at me.

"Come on, kids," I said holding the door for the ani-mals. Shasta bounced out of Misty's lap before she could get her door open, and met Roadkill crawling over the girl on the floor of the back seat.

Girl on the floor of the back seat.

"What the ever-loving fuck is this?" I yelled. She smiled up at me and crawled out of the car with the ani-mals. Her bright red hair was offset by the forest green of her leather clothes. They looked like they'd been made by the same tailor as Misty's. "Princess Bridget Rex," I sighed.

"Glad you stopped, Warrior Wizard. I have to go pee, too!"

The animals had already found a spot to relieve them-selves. Misty, Princess, and I rushed to the restrooms and each slammed a stall door shut behind us.

"OKAY, PRINCESS, SPILL it. Why are you hiding in the back of my car? And why the hell did you wait until we were nearly a hundred miles away to tell us, so now I have a good two-hour drive to get you back home and then start all over on our quest?"

"I'm going with you."

"No. That isn't even an answer to my question. No one invited you along and now I'll have half the Sovereignty out hunting me like your brother's kidnappers. Kidnappers! Do you get that?" I shouted.

"Nobody's going to hunt for you," she sighed. She opened her matching green leather purse and pulled out another sheet of paper to hand me. It was handwritten and I wondered if the girl had tried to disguise her own writing.

> *Know all by these presents:*
> *The Sovereign and First Lady grant their permission for their daughter, Princess Bridget Rex, to travel with the Wizard Warrior Jackie on her quest and to join in all such adventure as such quest might bring.*
> *This further appoints Wizard Warrior Jackie as temporary guardian of Princess Bridget Rex.*
> *Signed, Regina Elizabeth Rex, First Lady*

"This is conspicuously missing your father's signature, which I have several copies of so I could compare it," I said.

"Mother said you wouldn't notice that. So, please don't notice." I just stared at her with my mouth open.

"Why don't you two come and join me for a mid-morning snack," Misty said. She had a picnic basket sitting on one of the tables in the rest area and was unpacking what looked like a lot more than a snack. Now that she mentioned it, though, I was hungry. We went to sit at the table.

"Why would you want to go on a quest with us?" I asked as I took an egg salad sandwich and a cup of hot coffee from Misty. I put the question of where hot coffee came from away from my mind. It was all a dream. I was convinced.

"He's my brother."

"I watched you at breakfast yesterday. You didn't seem happy that we were going to go find him," I said. "A little sibling rivalry going on here? Are you hoping to stop us from finding him?"

"No! The little brat is a worthless dick, but he's my brother. I was unhappy about you being offered the reward."

"The reward? Your brother's hand in marriage? Believe me, that is never going to happen. What is he? Ten? No way, baby," I laughed. Even Misty rolled her eyes at that one.

"You made that clear at the table. Then Daddy dearest offered you half the Sovereignty."

"And you don't want me to have half the Sovereignty," I said. "Don't worry. Too much paperwork. Not interested."

"Fine, but if *I* bring back my brother, my father has to honor the agreement. He can't offer me the hand of my brother in marriage! Oh, yuck! So, he'd have to offer me half the Sovereignty. And I'm pretty sure I can talk my brother out of the other half." She set her coffee mug down with a decided thump. I glanced at it and saw that she had hot chocolate. I didn't even see a thermos around.

"So, what you want is the Sovereignty. Why don't you just support Valentine, marry him, and become First Lady?"

"Yu-uck! And I thought my brother would be a bad deal. Valentine is a weasel. And I'd have to be installed as First Lady for at least a year before I could poison him and get away with it. And through that whole year, I'd be losing handmaidens and pages who had to taste my food for me." The picture she painted of poisonings and attempted murders was shocking.

"Princess," Misty said nicely, "what skills do you have that will make you a valuable addition to our quest and not just an added burden? You have to know that Jackie has all she can do just to keep me out of danger. If she has to focus on you, either I'd get left out or she'd never be able to focus on her quest." Nicely put. I wanted to protest that Misty was no burden, but that would contradict her argument for getting rid of Princess.

"Unlike you," Princess said haughtily, "I'm actually trained in how to use my sword and defend my person with advanced martial arts. I have twelve other weapons concealed on my person, the greatest of which is my look of vulnerability and innocence."

Okay. That was almost too much. Maybe it's type-casting, but I have never met a redhead I considered either vulnerable or innocent. Think about it. Redhead. Innocent. Contradiction in terms. I swallowed the remains of my sandwich which seemed to have lasted a long time while I kept eating it. Before she could move or defend herself, I whipped the gold cord off my robe and looped it around her, holding her tight.

Princess dropped her head in submission.

"Yes, Warrior Wizard?" she said meekly.

"Now you listen carefully. If you are to join this quest, you will be the lowest person among us. If I tell you something, you do it. No questions asked. If Misty tells you to wash the dishes, you do it, immediately. If Roadkill makes you lie on the floor for the whole trip, you do it. Do you understand?"

"Yes, Warrior Wizard. I'll be good."

"When we enter into battle, your first responsibility is to stay safe, not to engage any enemy. When we recapture your brother, you will share the space with him and there will be no squabbling. When we return, you can make up any damn story you want to about how you rescued him and I'll support it so you get the reward. But until that time, you do what you're told. Understand?"

"Yes, Warrior Wizard." I removed the rope from around her and tossed it on with the other cords. "That wasn't fair," she whined.

"Is there a problem over here?" a voice said approaching the table. I turned and saw a policeman, complete with Smokey the Bear hat and uniform.

"No, officer," I said brightly. "My niece and I were just having a discussion about the merits of graduating at the top of her class. You know, kids can't get ahead unless they apply themselves."

"Don't I know it. Little miss, is this your aunt?"

"Um… Yes, officer."

"Are you traveling with her willingly?"

"Definitely."

"I have no other concerns. I just stopped to tell you that there is a late winter storm coming toward us fast. We're warning all travelers down off the pass and blocking traffic both directions. You folks should get a move on." He tipped his hat and turned to find other people in the rest area.

"Let's pack up and get moving," I said. "I've already had too many storms on this trip." Gray clouds were moving in fast and turning blacker as they blocked the sun. We ran to the car and I started it as Misty put away the picnic basket. Princess got the cat in her lap in the back seat as Roadkill took up the rest of the seat. As soon as Misty was back in the car, we turned out of the parking lot to head downhill.

MILE 540

BY THE TIME we'd gone a mile, we were being pelted with ice and snowflakes the size of baseballs. Huge wet things

I was afraid would dent the car. Progress slowed until we finally came out of the storm about ten miles down from the summit. I should say that we came out of the snow. It turned to rain, if not the deluge we'd experienced at Thunder Mountain, I slowed to a crawl in order to see clearly. I confess that I was subtly shifting my glance from side to side as I watched for monsters or, worse yet, snakes.

We came out on a fairly flat straight section of highway and the rain let up enough that we could get back near the speed limit in lighter rain. That lasted about twenty more miles.

"Oh, hey!" Misty said, looking at the TripTik. "Slow down. We're approaching a frontier."

"A what?"

"We're crossing into someone else's land," she explained. "Border patrol and customs."

"Damn. Get out our passports. Princess, do you have a passport?" I demanded as I slowed up.

"Of course," she answered. She dug in her leather bag and came up with a red passport, different from our blue ones. I rolled to a stop at the barrier gate and a well-armed guard approached the car. I cranked down the window.

"Passports," the guard said. I handed the three passports to the guard. He looked at them and backed away from the car, bringing his rifle down to bear. "Please all step out of the car," he said. There were suddenly about twenty rifles pointing at us, completely surrounding the car. I opened the door and kept my hands up where they could be seen as Princess shoved the seat forward and climbed out. Roadkill followed her. Misty and Shasta got out the other side. A more officious looking fellow came out of the guardhouse next to us. You could tell he was more important than the normal soldiers because he had a white belt that crossed his right shoulder and joined the one at his waist. I think they're called a Sam Browne belt, but basically, he looked like an elementary school crossing guard.

He took the passports as Misty and Shasta were led around the car to join us.

"You have a diplomatic passport," he said addressing Princess. "I assume these are just your escorts with bearer passports. To what does the land Anatnomia owe your visit?"

"As you very well know," Princess answered, "the only way to reach our southern range is through this corner of Anatnomia. Why anybody would block the road into our own land is beyond me."

"Well, Miss Princess Rex, I wouldn't know about that, would I?" he sneered. "Search the vehicle for contraband!" he snapped at his soldiers. I wondered what counted as contraband here. I was pretty sure something must. I racked my brain for some instruction for my weaponry that would be effective against twenty guards and wouldn't result in my immediate death. Mr. Officious reached over and took hold of my sword. Before it had cleared the scabbard, Roadkill started to growl and Shasta bristled. Surprisingly, he let the sword slide back into the sheath, but didn't let go. He looked into my eyes and I saw him begin to shrink before me.

I GUESS THE time has come when I gotta tell you a little about my eyes. This is going to be painful because it was something my mother told me when I was little. I was in maybe second grade and the teacher was giving us a diversity lesson. She had us all compare skin color so that we could see that even people we considered to be the same color we were, weren't. Skin tones were all over the place and it didn't matter what race we were. And then she had us compare hair color and eye color. To compare eye color, we had to line up by eye color, blue eyes first. Then we were going to all go down the row and describe each person's eye color with a description that wasn't just blue. She even had a box of 120 different crayons there that we could use for reference.

I was last in line and by the time I got to the first blue-eyed person to look at, everybody was laughing and having a good time. So, I stepped up to Debbie Warfield and she grinned and looked me right in the eye. I could see her eye-color change from something that was bright sky blue to a dark stormy blue and she started crying. Ms. Tomlinson, our teacher, came running over and wanted to know what I'd done to Debbie. I hadn't done anything and Debbie just pointed at my eyes. Ms. Tomlinson turned and looked into my eyes for a long time and I felt like I was being looked at inside. I saw her eyes were kind of greenish blue and the pupils contracted and got real small.

"I see," she said. She stood up rather stiffly and addressed the class. Everybody but me had finished going down the line. "We need to cut this lesson a little short," she said in her kind voice. Only it sounded a little stressed. "I've let the time get away from me because we were having so much fun. So, return to your seats and let's get started on our reading assignment."

When I got home, I ran to Mommy and told her all about the girl crying when she looked at my eyes. See this is the hard part, because Mommy was really nice to me and kind and I had no idea that one day she would kill my daddy. She got a mirror and told me to look deep in my own eyes and to describe to her what color they were. I said, "Brown."

"Look closely, now," she said. "Tell me what you see." I examined my eyes pretty close and maybe I saw what Debbie Warfield did. My eyes are brown, but there are streaks of black and gold shot through the irises. And as I looked, they shifted a little. Some got longer and some got shorter and then they'd pulse and go back the other way.

I was pretty confused, because at eight years old, I hadn't really looked deeply into that many eyes. I just assumed everyone had eyes like mine, but maybe they had different colors of streaks to match the dominant color of their eyes.

"I'll tell you something my grandma told me when I was little," Mommy said. "Once in every seven genera-tions or so, a woman shows up in our family with the witch-eye. I didn't believe any of the stories she told me about what a grandmother seven generations ago had done. But she warned me and I knew when I saw my baby's eyes that the witch-eye was present. She said some people could be bent to the will of a witch-eye and to be careful how I used it."

I can't tell you how I avoided looking people in the eye after that. But after a long while, nobody seemed to interact with me any different than anyone else, so I pretty much forgot about it and it's just one of those silly family legends that every family has. I knew a kid in fourth grade who claimed to be a distant relative of Billy the Kid, for example. We've all got those hidden stories that are passed down through our families.

So, I just wanted my eyes to be normal eyes with no special powers and it would be too terrible to think otherwise, because if I bent a person to my will by looking into his eyes, then that night I was making out with Dan Blackwell and I looked deep into his eyes and he took me to bed and took my virginity might have all been because I made him do it, and I couldn't stand thinking he didn't really want to.

"WE WERE PAID," Mr. Official said to me in a rasping voice. "Men from Victoriana came down from the pass just ten days ago. They said to watch for anyone coming with a bearer passport and stop them until they got here. The alarm went out as soon as your passport was opened. I don't know how soon they'll get here. You'd better leave now." He broke away from my eyes and let go of the sword, stepping away. "They're clear!" he called out to his men searching the car. "These aren't the ones we want." He handed back our passports and waved us back to the car.

> *These aren't the droids you're looking for. You*
> *can go about your business. Move along.*

We didn't waste any time getting ourselves back in the car. I checked to make sure we had everyone and the doors were all closed. As soon as the gate opened ahead of us, I headed through it.

"Turn right at the crossroad ahead," Misty called out as she looked at the TripTik. "Here!"

I hit the brake and we pretty much drifted around the corner. The road was straight and flat and I laid on the accelerator. First, I didn't trust the spell on that official—or whatever it was—to hold. He could be sending his soldier boys after us already. And two, if the Caesars were headed after us, I didn't want to wait around for them.

And I really didn't want to contemplate the power of my eyes.

Chapter 8

Run for the Border

"ANYTHING YOU'D LIKE to tell me about that little display at Customs?" I asked Princess. "Diplomatic passport?"

"Every member of the Sovereign family has a diplomatic passport," she replied. I waited. At the crossing, Misty and I had been relegated to the position of escorts for the royal brat. Finally, she sighed. "Mother was afraid you'd have trouble crossing the border, even with bearer passports. Maybe even because of the bearer passports. They aren't recognized everywhere. She thought if I was with you, they'd just wave us through."

"So, your mother was actually in on you stowing away and was really the one who signed your permission slip?" I asked.

"Yes. Did you think it was a forgery?" Princess asked, as if she was far above doing such a thing.

"It seemed suspicious and not very neatly put together."

"We were in a hurry."

"Fine. Let's see if your charm will get us through the border back into Victoriana. I assume that's where we're going," I said.

"The south crossing is a hundred miles from here. I'm going to sleep." Princess closed her eyes tightly and leaned back against the window. Shasta had abandoned Misty and lay in Princess's lap with Roadkill leaning his head against her. I reminded myself that she was only fifteen and I should make allowances for her being a kid.

Then I started to laugh. Misty looked at me strangely, but I couldn't even form a response to her question, "What?" I was only eighteen! If I was supposed to make allowances for a fifteen-year-old, who was making allowances for me? And the more I thought about Misty being the responsible adult among us, the funnier it got. I just shook my head and laughed.

I pressed the accelerator a little more firmly and our speed climbed toward ninety.

"I'VE GOT IT," Misty said as we raced down the road. This was by no means a superhighway. It was marked with two lanes, but we'd met no oncoming traffic. I'd passed a couple of slow moving vehicles, though.

"What'cha got?" I asked. I loved the feel of the muscle car now that I had let the horses out to run. It was made for this.

"The Belt and Sword of Truth," Misty said, holding the book of weapons open in her lap. She'd been researching what each of my weapons could do. We'd soon discovered that everything I wore was a weapon of some sort.

"That's not like that other Terry Goodkind book is it? That was so bloody. How many heads did that guy cut off?"

"Too many. But no. This is more like the biblical belt of truth and sword of the spirit. When the two are together, anyone who touches the hilt of the sword is compelled to tell the truth. You can place a person's hand on the hilt and as long as it's in the scabbard and attached to the belt, they have to answer any question truthfully. If the sword is out of the scabbard, it is able to detect deceit but not compel the truth."

"Well, that explains that," I said with finality. If it was the sword and belt I'd been given that compelled the border guard to tell the truth about why we were stopped, then it wasn't my eyes. Except for one niggling detail. When he grabbed my sword and looked in my eyes, he'd blurted out everything we needed to know and let us through. But I'd never asked him a question.

MILE 643

TRAFFIC PICKED UP both directions as crossroads became more frequent and we entered the outskirts of Anavic. Apparently, that was supposed to be a combination of Anatnomia and Victoriana—the border town. Misty was studying the TripTik but hadn't offered any directions, so I just kept on the main drag as traffic became downright congested. I saw a sign that said 'Pepe's Best Tacos' and swung off the street into a Mexican restaurant kind of place.

"Potty break. Let's have tacos for lunch," I said. Princess woke up and the animals stretched. Sorry. Didn't mean to make it sound like Princess was an animal. I don't think.

"Here! We're supposed to stop here," Misty said.

"Why no directions until after I was already parked?" I asked.

"It was doing stupid stuff," Misty complained. What kind of stupid stuff can a paper map do? "I'd start to say turn right, and the instructions would fade out. I'd look around and there was no place to turn. Then it would say stop here and there'd be no place to stop. It just all of a sudden settled with the words, 'Eat here.'"

"Maybe it only works in Victoriana," Princess volunteered. "The border shifts around a lot."

We traipsed into the little taco restaurant and I was pleased to find it was a real Mexican taco place like you'd get out of a truck on the sidewalk instead of a fast food taco place like the one that can't decide if it's tacos or fried chicken or pizza. It had a spicy smell that set my stomach rumbling.

"Your order?" The guy at the counter was looking at the emblem on my chest.

"Warrior Wizard," I answered. He looked up at me uncertainly.

"Warrior Wizard special!" he called to the kitchen. I waved Princess and Misty up to the counter and they ordered things that were actually on the menu. Misty shoved a card in the reader and the counter guy pushed a button to give her a receipt.

"Uh... Is this usual traffic out here?" I asked, looking out the front window at the long line of cars.

"Oh, sometimes. The border's closed and the army has traffic backed up for miles," he said.

"Why is it closed?" I asked.

"Oh, you know. Someone on one side farted and the other side thought they were shooting, so they stopped all the traffic and lined up on either side of the crossing with guns pointing at each other."

"Oh, Pepe, that story is as old as I am," Princess laughed.

"That may be," he said, "but now every time someone raises a stink at the border, we say it's closed because of farts. Sometimes it applies to the people in authority. Doesn't make any sense otherwise." A bell rang and he brought back our plates of food.

"What is this?" I asked, looking at the huge tortilla-wrapped roll on my plate.

"Warrior Wizard special: A super-size grande shredded pork and beans burrito," the proprietor said. I usually try not to eat anything bigger than my head, but this... I was going to take a stab at it. I cut a bite off it and savored the spicy meat and beans. "Four pounds," the proprietor stated proudly. This was going to take a while.

We finished our meal and I discovered my plate was empty. I'd even sopped up the extra sauce and cheese from my plate with another tortilla. I leaned back in my chair and looked out the window again, thinking maybe it was time for a siesta before we got back in line.

"Is there another way across the border?" I asked as he picked up our plates.

"Oh, sure. It's not legal, exactly."

"How exactly?"

"Well, my clientele comes from both sides of the border for Pepe's Best Tacos. So, all you really have to do is drive out the back of my parking lot and you're across the border."

"That easy? There's no fence?"

"They try to make me put up a fence. Why would I do that? I'd lose half my business. And if they want a fence, they can pay for it. I'm not paying to put a fence across my parking lot and prevent people from coming for my tacos." I looked at my companions. Even Shasta seemed to raise an eyebrow at me.

"Time to roll," I said.

We left the restaurant and piled into the Fairlane. True enough, there was no fence and the drainage ditch that marked the border was scarcely a depression as big as a speed bump. Once through the parking lot. Misty looked at the TripTik and pointed left. I turned right.

MILE 651

IT TOOK AN hour to get out of town. The traffic on this side of the border was backed up just as far, so we had to drive the wrong direction until we could make a turn and come back on a side street, then weave around a couple of traffic circles and into a residential neighborhood, before I could get pointed the right direction and pick up where the TripTik showed us.

By that time, we were all feeling the effects of the huge meal we ate.

"I need a bathroom," Princess said.

"Me, too," I answered. "I'll find one as soon as possible."

"And Roadkill just farted," she continued. I rolled down my window.

"Quick! Close the border," Misty laughed. Then she groaned as the smell reached the front seat. She quickly rolled down her window. Shasta jumped over the seat onto her lap and stuck her nose out the window.

As luck would have it, there was a park at the edge of Victanat, the sister city of Anavic. I pulled in and we all headed for the bathrooms, suggesting that Roadkill find someplace far away to do his business. When we'd all gathered back at the car, I opened the hatch and Misty pulled soft drinks from the cooler. There was a ball court nearby, so I grabbed my basketball and strolled over to shoot a few hoops. I was holding my Shasta Creme Soda in one hand while I launched the basketball with the other and dropped it through the hoop. Princess and Misty were lounging against the car with Shasta and Roadkill prowling around looking for gophers.

When it comes down to it, all I really want to do is play roundball. This Warrior Wizard stuff was getting old and I was truly considering waking myself up. It all had to be a dream, right? I guess I just got lost in the moment because the next thing I heard was a scream from near the car. I spun and saw four guys in dark suits grabbing Misty and Princess. I palmed the basketball and pitched it as hard as I could. I hit the guy on my left and he went reeling backward into the parking lot. Shasta and Roadkill were on top of the other guy and Misty was free. I turned toward Princess just in time to see her shoved in the back of a van by one guy. The other had disappeared.

I didn't even hesitate. I pulled my mortarboard off my head and used a side-arm throw. It lodged just below his ribs and he fell to the ground as the van door slid closed and he peeled out of the parking lot. As I ran toward the Fairlane, I scooped the basketball up off the ground. I could see the guy I'd knocked down was the big burly guy who threatened us at the hotel in East Love. The side of his face looked more like I'd thrown a burning bowling ball at him than a basketball. I spent a whole second trying to feel sorry for him. The other guy, still cowering in a fetal position while Shasta paced around him, had a patch over one eye. Misty opened her car door and got in. Shasta leapt into her lap and she slammed the door shut. I ran to the other side of the car and when I opened the door, Roadkill trotted up with my mortarboard and jumped in the back seat. I tossed the basketball in with him.

I handed the cap to Misty and turned the ignition. When the big engine roared to life, I popped the clutch and we spun out of the parking lot in hot pursuit of the van. I could see it half a mile ahead of us. Misty wiped the blood off the corner of my hat and handed it back to me, then calmly opened the TripTik.

"We won't need that as long as I can see that SOB ahead of us," I said. Misty laughed. "What?" I barked.

"The TripTik just says, 'Follow that van!'"

"Great. Now we have a smartass paper GPS." I pressed the accelerator almost to the floor and we started closing the distance to the van.

MILE 670

WE HAD COME down from a mountain pass getting into Anatnomia. It looked like the route into Victoriana was up and over the mountains again. The road was twisting and switched back on itself at times so tightly that I could see the van out my side window as it passed on the next curve. There was only so much speed I could pour on here. The van couldn't do better. I could see it lean dangerously around a curve as it was.

"Does this road ever straighten out?" I called to Misty.

"This shows a half-mile straight stretch up to the pass and another half-mile on the other side. Then it gets all twisty again."

I rounded the next curve and saw the straightaway in front of me and floored the Fairlane. It responded by jumping ahead and in a second or two, I was beside the van and Valentine Caesar was looking out in terror. There was a rest area viewpoint at the top of the pass and I moved the Fairlane into the side of the van to force it off the road and into the park. It bumped over a curb and came to rest against a picnic table. I stopped a little less suddenly and we piled out of the car. Before we got to the van, Valentine was standing beside it with Princess in his grasp and a knife held to her throat.

"Don't come any closer!" he shouted. "I don't want to hurt her, but I will if you force me. Since you wrecked my van, we'll just have to take your car. I have both brats now and nothing can stop me being named the successor."

I jammed a hand in my pocket trying to find anything I could use without a sudden movement. The only thing I found was a handful of beans. Magic beans. I pulled one slowly from my pocket and started to calm the guy down with soothing hand motions with one hand as I brought the other up as if to wipe my eye. I lodged the bean between my thumb and index finger.

"We won't interfere. The keys are in the car. There's lots of food in back. You're leaving us with nothing to get by on. That's really mean," I complained. He started to laugh at that and edge toward the car. As soon as his eyes flicked toward the open door, I flicked the bean at him. *"Ne bouge pas!"* I shouted. The bean hit his hand and he froze. I walked over and pried the knife from his immobile fingers. As soon as the pressure was away from her, Princess wiggled out of the arms of the frozen man and threw herself at me, crying like a frightened two-year-old. Misty came and pulled her away from me to comfort while I dealt with the wayward Caesar.

I pulled the light blue cord from around my neck and wrapped it around him.

"I don't know how long the don't move spell lasts," I said. "But I don't think I should leave you here unable to defend yourself in case wild animals come prowling around." I flicked a finger at him and said, *"Libérer."* His hand dropped to his side and he looked around frantically, but still unable to move while he was bound by my light blue cord.

"Don't hurt me. Please, don't hurt me," he pled with tears in his eyes. "I didn't mean anything. I'd never really hurt her."

"Ha!" Princess barked. That was followed by a well-placed kick to his crotch. His eyes crossed and he would have doubled over had he not been bound by the cord. I could see the raw hatred in his eyes.

"Honest. They made me do it. My grandfather. He thinks your father stole the Sovereignty from him. This whole thing is his idea." He tested the bonds of the cord briefly but shrank away from me when I drew my sword. Misty and Princess followed suit and he had three swords and two snarling animals facing him as I released the bond.

"I'd take you with me, but we're already a little crowded in the Fairlane. Get in the van and buckle yourself in," I commanded. He obeyed and I pulled another bean from my pocket and slammed it against the door. *"Serrure!"* I commanded. All the doors in the van locked. "We'll send a tow truck for you from the next town we see. Mount up, kids. Let's get out of here." We all ran to the car and jumped in. Shasta and Roadkill were on either side of Princess in the back seat, licking her face. I'd left the car running when we all jumped out, so I just put it in gear and moved out. I looked in the rearview mirror and could see Valentine struggling to get a window open while he waved a gun around. I hadn't thought about that possibility. I floored it and was out of sight by the time I heard the shot ring out.

MILE 793

I DIDN'T LET any grass grow under our tires getting down from the pass. I stopped at a gas station in a little town at the foot of the pass and told them a guy in a van was stuck on the pass. I looked at the name on the station. 'Little Caesar's.' I didn't smell pizza. "I think the guy up there is one of yours, so you might want to go get him before the wild animals do." I checked the gas gauge, noting it was still full, and headed out of town. I didn't know if there were wild animals up on the pass, but it seemed to get the guys in motion and headed away from me.

"You okay, kiddo?" I asked.

"You came to my rescue. I was kind of a bitch and you still saved me."

"Yeah. Kinda. So, you're okay?"

"I guess so. I just feel like I caused you a whole lot of problems you didn't need. I'm sorry," she said. She hugged Roadkill in the back seat and Shasta started purring in her lap loud enough to be heard over the motor.

"Your father's going to owe me a paint job on my car if there's a scratch on it," I said. "Pop would kill me if I bring it home scratched."

"Uncle Harry owns a body shop in East Love. He'll take care of it."

"Let me get this straight. The brother of the Sovereign is a body mechanic?"

"Yeah. So what?"

"Just trying to wrap my head around this strange little land of yours. What's the lay of the land ahead, Misty? We'll probably need a place to stay for the night."

"The TripTik says we're still headed kind of southwest. It doesn't ever seem to show anything until I turn a page or something. The big map doesn't show the road, but if we assume that the road somehow connects these regions, I'd say... there's nothing but a couple little villages. Looks like we'll need to find a campsite eventually."

"Princess, reach behind you and grab a bag of chips, please," I said. "Looks like we'll be on the road a while and I'm hungry."

"Are you always hungry?" she asked. "Seems like we've stopped four times for food already and it's only early afternoon." Her attitude was beginning to return and I figured that was a good sign. She twisted in the seat and reached below the cover to grab a bag of chips and hand them forward. Misty tore the bag open with her teeth and held it out for me to grab a few. I didn't remember hanging onto it, but the remains of my creme soda was in the cup holder.

"So, anything you can tell us about the territory we're headed into?" I asked.

"Not much. Most of it is wild until we get around the big lake and head back north," Princess said. She leaned forward and pointed out the features on the map to Misty. Misty read the legends on the map.

"Werewolves?" she said. "Really?"

"There's said to be a small pack of them. They don't show up much, though," Princess said. I saw her shiver in the rearview mirror.

"Oh, well," I said. *Werewolves. Right.* "Find us some music, hon."

Soon the sounds of k.d. lang were filling the car and we were all howling:

Ooooooooooooooo
won't someone save me
from that full moon full of love

Roadkill and Shasta joined right in. I guess before bed tonight, I was going to check to see what phase the moon was in.

"I'M TIRED. EVERYBODY needs to pee. We need a campsite. Mapmaker, mapmaker, make me a map, find me a place where I can nap," I sang. Misty flipped open the TripTik.

"Mount Morrisey Park, on the left in... Slow down! Two hundred yards!" Misty yelled. I slammed on the brakes, thankful the pavement was dry. I saw the sign for the park just as I slowed enough to make the turn. "Um... site seventeen."

We drove into the park and scouted around until we saw campsite number seventeen. Wouldn't you know. It had my WW logo on the post.

This campground was quite different than the first one we used. There were people here. In fact, almost every campsite had someone in it. I backed in next to the tent site and everybody got out of the car, rubbing their collective asses. The vibration of the engine could be felt in my feet, even after I was standing on solid ground.

"We should get camp set up, I suppose," I said. "Ever done any camping out, Princess?"

"Ha! I was a Senior Girl Guide. I could make camp with nothing but what I have on my person," Princess said.

"Well, even though that would be interesting to see, we have a tent," Misty said. "Catch." Misty tossed the tent over to Princess and she staggered back a step, scowling at my aunt.

"Very funny. Where do you want it?" Princess asked.

I pointed to the obvious bare flat spot and reached into the back of the car to get out the cooler and sleeping bags. When I turned around, the tent was up.

"That was fast!"

"Sometimes, we needed to outrun a storm and get camp set up before we got soaked," Princess said smugly.

"Oh, this is nice," a man said approaching our camp. "A Warrior Wizard to join our party tonight." He motioned a couple other men and a woman closer with him. They didn't look all that respectable, but what did I know about the customs in this part of the land?

"I'm Jackie," I said. "You folks camped here, too?"

"Yeah. Going to catch one tonight, we are," the guy said.

"We've never had a Warrior Wizard join the hunt," the woman said.

"The hunt?" I asked. "We just got here to spend the night because there were no hotels around. Plan to have some food and go to sleep."

"If you sleep, you'll be food," the other man said. "It's full moon tonight and a clear sky. The werewolves can't help coming close."

"Oh, crap! You mean actual werewolves are coming out and you're going to fight them?"

"Yeah. You wouldn't believe what a good fight we can have. We've got Charlie staked out as bait. Unless you want to offer these two. Charlie is none too happy about having lost the lotto. That little redhead would make a tasty morsel to attract a wolf."

"My companions are not bait. Do you really mean you stake out a human being as bait for wolves? I assume you rush out to defend him then?" I couldn't believe what I was hearing.

"Well, we do our best, but bait is bait. Sometimes it gets taken. But the price of a pelt is worth the risk."

"Is it really?" Misty asked. "What weapons do you fight with?"

"The usual. Slingshots and knives. Raymond has a sword and Matilda, here, got some wolfsbane that she's tipped arrows with. The big thing is to not let them break through into the camp. So, come and join us at moon-rise. You must have some magic you can use against a werewolf. Or he could get *you!*" The asshole jumped toward me with his hands held like claws. It was almost the last thing he did as Roadkill was on him and knocked him flat, snarling and growling.

"Help! Get him off!" Matilda said. "He didn't mean anything by that. He was just having a little scare on you."

"Roadkill, here!" I commanded. My dog jumped to me, prancing in his fancy blue vest and spike collar. "It looks like his little scare backfired." The guy, who never offered his name, scrambled backwards and got to his feet, pointing at Roadkill.

"That animal attacked me!"

"You won't last long against a werewolf if my little mutt scares you that badly," I laughed. "Thanks for the invitation. We're going to build a fire and make dinner now. Bye!" I waved at them as they scattered back toward their own campsites where fires were already burning. I turned to getting one built in the site fire pit. There was a stack of wood next to it. I'd worry about replenishing the supply in the morning.

"What are you going to do, Jackie?" Princess asked. "Werewolves are nothing to sneer at. They can be really vicious. Wolf baiting like this was banned years ago. Maybe we should sleep in the car."

"Might not be a bad idea," Misty said. "At least put the animals in the car. They might attack to defend us and get injured." My sweet aunt had her priorities straight. Don't let the pets get injured defending us.

I nodded. But it was stupid to let all these people face the danger with knives, swords, and poison-tipped arrows. I went to the car and opened the passenger door. I reached into the glovebox and pulled out the gun we'd been given when we broke up the robbery. I hoped it had some ammunition in the clip.

"You have a gun?" Princess whispered, shocked. I nodded and ejected the clip to see how many cartridges were left. "Sure hope you have some silver bullets."

I just stood there and stared at her.

Chapter 9

Howl at the Moon

I SAT IN THE PASSENGER SEAT with the gun in my lap while Misty and Princess busied themselves with getting dinner ready. I carefully examined the gun and ejected the magazine. I operated the slide to be sure there was no shell in the chamber. There was and I caught the ejected shell to examine. No. It definitely wasn't silver. I emptied the magazine—a total of eight bullets. None of them were silver.

Silver bullets didn't enter the canon of werewolf lore until the mid-twentieth century, though there are hints about the toxicity of silver to werewolves from earlier than that. Contemporary stories all seemed to agree that it takes a silver weapon to kill a werewolf, since if you are close enough to cut off its head or remove its heart, you are probably already dead. This according to Misty's vast fantasy lore. Well, I read *Twilight* and *Harry Potter*, too. I wondered if the werewolves of Mount Morrisey Park were like that poor professor Lupin who was bitten by a werewolf in a battle and therefore became one. I started searching through the various manuals we'd found hidden among my travel documents.

A Catalogue of Dangers was included, so I looked up werewolves in the booklet. I kept getting distracted by other dangers listed, including poison berries, poison snakes, poison insects, and mountain monsters, variously described as anything from Bigfoot to an ogre. But no werewolves. I went flipping back through the pages trying to find out about 'killing' and thinking that article might have some specific instructions based on what needed killing. Nothing. I turned the page and there it was.

> **Lycanthrope**. *A werewolf. In ancient mythology and contemporary literature, it is said to be a human that transforms to a wolf, usually under the light of a full moon. However, in Victoriana, the Lycanthrope is a highly intelligent and vicious beast, most commonly identified as a wolf, but may take the form of any large carnivorous animal. Its voracious appetite and aggressiveness are at their peak during a full moon. If at all possible, avoid contact. If necessary to engage in combat, the most effective weapon is a silver bullet. Other silver weapons may also be effective, by severing the head or piercing the heart. Fire can be an effective defense.*

Okay. I'm back to silver. Silver bullet, silver sword, silver knife, silver spear. I'd noticed, however, that every entry in the booklet included the sage advice to avoid contact if possible.

"SO, IN THE stories you've heard, does a werewolf bite result in the bitten person becoming a werewolf?" I asked Princess as we sat eating an excellent meal of chicken cacciatore and garlic bread. I rather thought it was vampires that garlic was effective against, but I could smell garlic being cooked all over the campground.

"Um... As far as I know, a werewolf bite results in the bitten person becoming dinner. No one's ever survived," Princess said. That was encouraging.

"How does one become a werewolf then?" I continued.

"One is born a werewolf. One doesn't become one," she mocked me.

"Does a silver bullet kill it instantly?"

"Only if you hit it in the head or heart. Otherwise, it just stops the animal's ability to heal. It will die eventually, but it can do a lot of damage beforehand," Princess said. She had adopted a tone of teaching an elementary student in a classroom full of dunces. I appealed to Misty.

"Is a werewolf subject to magic? Like to Jackie's cord of submission?" she asked. Now that was a thought. All I'd need to do is get close enough to loop the gold cord around the wolf and it would obey me. The entire problem with that would be getting close enough without dying.

"As far as I know, the magic that might be effective against a werewolf would be an enchanted object. Something that it might do to itself, like putting the gold cord around its own neck after it's eaten you."

Great. This was all just great. But there were other enchantments. I thought about turning the bullet silver if I could remember the French for 'silver bullet.' Madam Auclair said something about what it meant. I pulled a bullet from my pocket and looked at it in the palm of my hand. 'Focus,' I thought to myself.

"Miracle," I said pointing at the bullet. I could be fooling myself, but I thought it glowed a little.

"Why are you asking for a miracle?" Misty said. "We could still just get in the car and drive away."

"It's French for silver bullet," I said.

"That's a metaphorical silver bullet," Misty said, shaking her head. "You need to transform it into an actual silver bullet."

I concentrated some more, thinking about what I needed. I reached in my pocket and pulled out the rest of the bullets. When I deposited them in my hand next to the other, I noticed I'd collected a bean, too. *A magic bean.* And I wanted a transformation, not a command. What was that story about the *papillon*? I had it!

"*Se métamorphoser en argent balles,*" I said emphatically. And that's when I got my miracle. The bean dissolved into dust and spread across the bullets. They glowed, and when the light subsided, I had eight silver bullets in my hand. "Yes!" I shouted triumphantly. Misty and Princess both jumped to look over my shoulder.

"Not bad for someone who doesn't believe in magic," Misty laughed.

"Holy wow! You just turned the bullets to silver. Will they still shoot?" Princess asked. The little bitch.

"Of course. I think. I just have to hit what I'm shooting at. In the heart or the head," I sighed. "Um... Keep the fire burning while I'm gone. I read that fire is also an effective defense against werewolves. Look, all the other campsites have bright fires burning." I loaded the cartridges in the magazine and shoved it in the gun. Hoped I'd done all that right. I read a thriller and the agent was always sure to put one in the chamber. I slid the slide and hoped that did the trick. I found the safety lever and practiced flicking it off and on with my thumb.

The sun was down and the noise from the other campsites was up. It was nearly moonrise. I tossed the car keys to Misty.

"If there's a sign of any of the creatures getting near, get in the car and drive away. Don't wait for me," I said.

"I can't drive," Misty said.

"Oh, geez! Give them to me. I can drive," Princess said.

"I'm not sure you could even reach the pedals," I said. "But if the time comes, Misty will give you the keys. Make sure Roadkill and Shasta are safe." I didn't give them time for any sappy goodbyes. I just stood up and headed toward the hunting ground with the gun tucked into my belt. With luck, these folks all knew what to do and I wouldn't be needed at all.

TWENTY SECONDS ON the edge of the gathering of would-be hunters and I was disabused of that opinion. There were twenty or twenty-five of them standing around with their knives and swords and pitchforks. Mabel had a bow and arrows, and someone was testing the pull of his slingshot. Most of them were dressed in some kind of armor, like having cookie sheets strapped to their chests and football helmets on.

And most of them were drunk, including the 'bait' they were gathered around. The guy—Charlie, they said—had an ankle shackle on with a chain attached to a stake in the ground.

"Don't you worry, none, Charlie. We're all right here beside you. Them wolves won't have a chance. Ernie has his dogs ready as soon as the critters show their faces. We'll take 'em down one right after another."

"There isn't really a need to have me chained here, Ross. I get the whole bait idea. But I'd like to be involved in the killing, too."

"If ya weren't chained, they'd know it was a trap. Smart critters these werewolves are."

"Yeah, well, still…"

A howl in the darkness brought everyone's head up. The full moon had just cleared the ridge to the east of us and it set the wolves to howling. I tried to identify how many there were by the number of howls and different directions they came from, but I couldn't separate them all. They were definitely getting closer. People started falling back in a half-circle behind Charlie, toward the campground.

"You all, don't just leave me out here," Charlie yelled. "You gotta be close."

"We're here, old buddy. Just need to give them some room to show themselves." It sounded like that voice was a lot farther away than was reasonable. I maintained my position where I'd stayed in the shadows. The next howl was much closer.

A shot whistled through the air and hit a tree on the far side of the clearing. I wondered if the guy had silver pellets for his slingshot.

"Don't waste your ammo, Cecil. Wait till you see the whites of their eyes."

"You don't need to wait," Charlie screamed. "Get 'em now! I can smell their breath!"

I doubted that, but a few more projectiles were thrown toward the edge of the clearing in the direction of the howls. At this rate, they wouldn't have anything to fight with by the time the wolves got close enough to see.

And then a yellow glint broke the circle of trees and a wolf crept into the open.

"There it is!" Charlie shouted. He was at the end of his tether. "Don't wait for whites of his eyes! They're yellow. Come on and get it now." An arrow flew through the clearing and buried itself in the ground about ten feet away from the wolf. It didn't even look toward it. I wondered how far away Mabel was with her bow.

Three more sets of eyes separated from the trees and crept toward the bait. My fingers itched on the gun, but I knew damn well that making a shot at all would take a passel of luck. I stood no more of a chance at this distance than Mabel did. The wolves moved forward and a bunch of things were launched at them. More slingshot. Rocks. A couple of knives. I think I saw a sword or a bayonet fly toward the wolves, all landing wide or short.

"You guys! You're too far away. You gotta come up here closer," Charlie screamed.

Suddenly three hounds came charging into the circle and began growling and snapping toward the wolves. The big wolf in the center stretched himself out and howled a long angry call. That was when I heard the first car door slam and an engine start. Someone had decided to abandon the fight.

"Don't go! Don't leave me here!" Charlie screamed. He was frantically tugging at his chain and rocking the stake back and forth in the ground. A dog leapt at the lead wolf as they closed in and the big wolf simply batted it aside with a massive paw. The hound lay on the ground twitching as another wolf approached to put it out of its misery with a bite to the neck. The other two dogs turned tail and ran, yelping all the way. I heard more doors slam and engines start. The hunt—and Charlie—was being abandoned. Well, the guy was an idiot, but I wasn't going to just leave him there to his fate. I raised the gun as the big wolf snarled and started forward with the other three trailing just slightly.

The echo of the shot I fired was louder than I expected. I hit the creature in the hind quarters and the howl he gave was much different than the hunting howl. The other three wolves turned their attention toward me, cautiously trying to circle me. Charlie started desperately rocking the stake back and forth as I took aim on the next wolf and fired.

It was a body shot and looked like I might have hit the vital organ with my silver bullet. The other two wolves jumped aside as I swung the gun around and they disappeared into the trees. I turned my attention to Charlie and helped him pull the stake from the ground. He started scrambling back, dragging the chain behind him.

That was the cue for the big bad wolf I'd shot first to shake his head and get to his feet. He was only a few feet away, but my hand was shaking now and my next shot didn't touch him. He sprang.

I lost my grip on the gun and my senses at the same time. I'm not sure what transpired because it was all reflex. What I know is that when I finished, I held my silver stole in my hand. Only it wasn't a stole any longer. It was a long, stiff broadsword of solid silver. The wolf lay dead in front of me with its head severed from its body, the dying light of his yellow eyes glaring balefully at me. I raised my head toward the moon and howled.

"OwowowooooooOw!" I screamed. The call was answered by retreating voices in the darkness.

I picked up the gun where it lay and threw the sword over my shoulder, where it draped like a stole. I walked back to our campsite. The rest of the sites were abandoned, fires still burning. Misty and Princess stood by our fire. Misty had a struggling Shasta in her arms and Princess held Roadkill's leash. When they saw me, they let go of their grip and the two animals rushed to me, Roadkill, licking at my hands and Shasta jumping all the way to my shoulder.

I sat next to the fire and Princess fetched a wet cloth with which she started mopping the blood from my robe. Misty busied herself at the fire and soon handed me a cup of cocoa, which I sipped thankfully. Then I saw she had one of the Scarecrow's blunts in her fingers and was lighting it. She took a toke and handed it to me. I took a long drag and held the smoke in my lungs. I looked at her and handed the joint to Princess. She looked a little uncertain, but sucked the smoke in and immediately started coughing her lungs out. That was usually Misty's province, but we rescued the joint and each managed a couple more drags before it vanished. I drank down the rest of my cocoa.

"You always know just what we need, Aunt Misty," I said.

"Right now, we need to go to bed. Look, the sky has clouded over. There won't be any more werewolves tonight." She said it calmly, as if she were an expert on the subject. I crawled into the tent and pulled off my boots and robe and hat. Misty crawled in beside me on one side and Princess on the other. Roadkill took his position across the entrance as Misty zipped it closed. It was too crowded in the bedroll, so Shasta curled up on top of me and we all went to sleep.

MILE 902

IN THE MORNING, Princess and I walked down to the battle site with Roadkill. Shasta stayed glued to Misty as she made breakfast. I wasn't sure what I expected to see. Since it was just a dream, I figured it would be a pleasant little clearing all covered with green grass. Not so. Nor was there the carnage that a normal person would have expected.

There was a dug-up hole where the stake in the ground had been and we could see where it was dragged toward the campground. And there were two large charred spots on the ground where the two wolves had been killed. I didn't exactly remember setting them on fire, but I did remember them burning. Princess examined the spots carefully and picked a bit of silver out of each charred spot. She stared at them and then handed them to me. They were mostly still bullet shaped, but had melted some. I dropped them in my medicine bag.

Suddenly, I had a sobbing girl clutching me. I wasn't sure what inspired this, but she was shaking and all I could do was hold her and comfort her.

"Thank you for coming back," she sobbed. "And thank you for not trading me for that poor guy who was staked here. We saw him drive out in a battered pickup truck just before the last howl. Knew it was him, because the stake was still hanging out his door on a chain. I was so afraid that I caused you to be hurt or killed because you'd have made better time without me and without having to chase my abductor across the mountain and without me having to stop and pee or eat or anything. I shouldn't have come. You really don't have a use for me."

"Hey there. Without you, who would have told me I needed silver bullets?"

"But you might not have even needed them." She handed me my car keys. "Here. I couldn't use them."

"What?"

"Misty gave them to me and told me to go ahead and leave because she and the animals wouldn't leave you behind. And... And that's when I realized, I couldn't leave you behind either. So, we just kept hold of Roadkill and Shasta and waited by the fire for you to come back," she said. "Um... We had a couple of stick bundles with the ends in the fire just in case we needed torches."

We walked back through the abandoned campsites. They'd left everything and I figured they'd be coming back later in the morning to see the results of the night's carnage. We didn't need to be around for that. But some of the huge campfires they had were still glowing embers, so we grabbed a couple of pans we saw and got water to pour over the coals and make sure they were dead out.

Misty had breakfast and coffee ready for us and I gave my aunt the same kind of huge hug Princess had given me. We cleaned up the campsite and were on the road in half an hour.

"IT WAS THE only weapon I had!" Charlie was saying to a group at the little café where we stopped for a mid-morning coffee. "That big monster of a wolf was on me like stink on shit. I pulled the stake out of the ground and drove it through his heart. Then I took off. That Warrior Wizard wasn't worth anything. Probably find her guts scattered about the place when we go out there."

Someone at his table noticed I'd walked into the café and went to the counter to order coffee. The café got suddenly quiet.

"Is that the way it happened Warrior Wizard?" One of the guys hollered. I thought it was Ernie from the night before. I turned and looked at the table. Charlie turned to look at me with terror etched on his face. I smiled.

"I reckon what happened after you all turned tail and ran, leaving your buddy as a sacrifice, is Charlie's story to tell. You listen to him and think about whether you should be staking people out for a werewolf hunt again." I turned away to pay for the three cups of coffee as Misty and Princess came out of the restroom.

"I know she got at least a couple of shots off from her gun. I bet she was shooting silver bullets and there isn't a werewolf left out there. And just as I was getting out of Dodge, there was a bloodcurdling howl. I thought it was the wolf, but I bet it was her."

We left, got back in the car, and drove away. Let Charlie tell the story the way he wanted to remember it. Maybe that would keep the nightmares away.

MILE 1076

WE PULLED INTO the town of Amherst. My first impression was that this was a normal sounding name for a normal looking town. There were several businesses along the main street through town that had the typical signs in the windows. You know the "4-day sale" and "Trucker's Special Breakfast" signs.

"TripTik has the Hotel a la Mode circled up here on the right," Misty said.

"Doesn't seem very urgent to move us on, does it?" I speculated. "Wonder why it wants us here. Where's the kid held from here?"

Misty switched maps and Princess leaned over the seat to look, too.

"Farther northwest, but it's impossible to tell the scale of things. We've been driving a couple hundred miles along this lake and it hardly looks like a blip on the map. But we got all the way from over here to the lake in just a couple of hours. So, short answer is, I don't know."

"Well, let's go register for a room and get a nice hot shower. As nice a job as Princess did wiping up the blood last night, I should really scrub this robe some more. And there's a red tinge around the edge of my stole." We got out of the car and started toward the hotel. Then we all stopped and looked up and down the street. There wasn't a car there. There wasn't a person in sight. We couldn't hear a thing moving or a bird singing.

"This is a little spooky," Princess said. Shasta and Roadkill both rubbed against us and followed us into the hotel with their heads against our legs. No one was in the lobby, so I went over to the desk and rang the bell. Nothing. I rang again.

I could hear a shuffling from the back and saw an eye and forehead peek around the corner. It looked for a few seconds and then was joined by the body of a young woman in a hotel reception uniform or something. She shuffled up behind the desk.

"May I help you?" she squeaked in a very soft voice.

"Our TripTik said this was a good place to stop for the night. Do you have a room available?" I asked. She looked surprised and then gave a little snort.

"You've got to be kidding! For a dollar and a ride out of town, I'll sell you the whole hotel," she said. "Why would you want to stay here? You should just keep driving. There's nothing here."

"Uh... We noticed there didn't seem to be anyone around. Where did everyone go?" Misty asked.

"Go? They're all right here." She waved a hand vaguely around the room.

"Well, if you can give us a room with a soft bed and a hot shower, and direct us to a good dinner, we'd gratefully appreciate it," I said.

"Your funeral." She checked us in and handed me the key.

"What about dinner?" I asked.

"Dining room opens at sundown," she said, smiling sweetly. That really wasn't comforting.

"Hon, let's bring the cooler in with us. I'm not sure I'm up for a restaurant meal tonight," Misty whispered to me. We went to the car and grabbed our packs and the cooler and made our way to the room. After a hearty meal that we found heated as soon as the cover was taken off, we all fell asleep on the two beds. We'd been up late and were drained from the previous night and nearly three hundred miles on the road during the day. It was only four-thirty in the afternoon and I allowed the bed to claim me.

I WAS AWAKENED by Roadkill whining beside the bed. When I stirred, Misty stirred, and when Misty stirred, Princess stirred, and that meant Shasta was stretching on top of us. I wondered when Princess had gotten in the same bed as the rest of us, but I couldn't blame her.

"You need to go out, fella?" I asked. Roadkill trotted over to the door and Shasta jumped out of bed to join us. "I'll be back in a few minutes," I said. "Gotta take the animals out."

"We'll get showers and get some more food ready," Misty yawned. Sounded like a good idea. I hadn't even taken my robe off when I lay down. I grabbed my hat and opened the door.

This was an old hotel in a small city. It was only five stories tall and being on the top floor still wasn't a hardship to use the stairs. The animals ran down in front of me and by the time I reached the third floor, I could hear voices below. Well, someone had come around, apparently. The voices got louder and when I reached the lobby, I saw into the dining room where a good number of people were seated and chatted as they ate. The food looked good, but something felt off. I stepped out the front with my animals.

We walked the entire length of the main drag—about six blocks—then turned and came back on the other side of the street. Everywhere we looked there were people going about their business. All the shops seemed to be open. I considered grabbing a cup of coffee at a little café, but decided to just make one up in our room. After all, Misty and Princess were preparing dinner. People seemed friendly enough, smiling and nodding as we passed, but I couldn't shake the feeling that something was off. For one thing, Roadkill and Shasta weren't responding to the people or noises at all. We finally got back to the hotel and went in to the sound of laughter and a band tuning up in the dining room. Hmm. Live music with dinner. Wondered what they'd play.

I stopped at the front desk and the young woman who checked us in was still working there. Long shift, I guess.

"The place looks a lot livelier this evening," I said casually. "Where were all these people earlier in the day?" She looked at me a long moment as if she couldn't believe I'd even asked.

"You're not much of a Warrior Wizard, are you?" she asked. I just shrugged and she sighed. "This is a ghost town."

Chapter 10

Ghost Town

"**O**H, THAT'S SO COOL!" I said. "You did the whole town!" I realized now what I'd been missing on our walk. If I'd paid attention to the animals, I'd have known much more quickly. There were no smells. The coffee shop didn't smell like coffee. The bakery didn't smell like anything baking. And there was an entire populated dining room just across the lobby and not a whiff of food or cooking aroma. I wondered for an instant if the desk clerk was part of the display, but she had substance. I could remember her handling Misty's credit card in the machine.

The look on her face was priceless.

"You like it?"

"Oh, yeah! It's great! I've got to run upstairs and tell Misty and Princess. They'll love it! Can we, like, actually go into the dining room and participate? Is it interactive?"

"Um... I guess so. We can even serve food, but it will take me a few minutes to change to my cook outfit."

"Sure, you go ahead. Let's make a reservation for... Let's say 9:30. That will give me time to take a shower. See you then!" I always liked haunted houses. The fact they'd built an entire haunted town was just a knock-out.

Roadkill, Shasta, and I took the stairs two at a time, all the way to the fifth floor.

I about died laughing when I walked into the room. Princess and Misty were shrunk up into a little ball together beside the bed. They were fixated on the wall across the room. I looked over there and saw a life-size scene playing out of a couple, apparently on their honeymoon. I had a feeling this could get racy.

"Isn't this cool?" I asked.

"But... They're... I mean..." Misty stuttered.

"Ghosts!" Princess blurted out. They turned and grinned at her, but didn't leave their little area on the far side of the room.

"Yeah, neat, huh? It's a whole ghost town. They're all over. It's better than that Haunted Mansion thing at Disney. It's the whole town. We've got a reservation for dinner. I need a shower first." I headed toward the bathroom.

"But but but... There's a body in the bathtub!"

"You're kidding! Just freakin' awesome!" I went into the bathroom and, just as they said, there was someone there. She wasn't just a body, though. She was taking a bath. You could see the water dripping off of her as she washed, but the tub was dry. She looked startled when she saw me. "Carry on," I said joyfully. "I'm just going to get a quick shower and then you can go back to what you were doing." I turned on the water to get it the right temperature and stripped out of my robe, undies, boots, and socks. The water was perfect, so I stepped in. Sort of stepped on her, but I did say sorry. She scooted toward the end so I'd have room without standing in her. The shower made her flicker a little, which only enhanced the realism in my mind. The door opened and Misty stuck her head in.

"You're really showering? In there? With her?" Misty croaked.

"Well, it's not like she takes up any space. Look! I think she's enjoying the water coming down." Indeed, the image was lifting her face to the spray and had a look of bliss on her face. Man, the folks who put this together really got it! "I'm getting out. You want me to leave the water running?" I asked.

"I'm good!" Misty squeaked. "No. I mean. Just fine. I'll just wait out here with Princess."

I turned off the water and stepped out of the shower. The towels were even warm. The girls didn't know what they were missing by not jumping into this shower. I looked at the tub. The image was sitting back down in it. She was looking mournfully up at the shower head.

"I don't really think I should just leave the shower on," I said. "I bet most people just see you in here and freak out like Misty and Princess did. Man, what they were missing! Tell you what. I assume you all disappear at sunrise like you appeared at sunset. I'll get up early and take another shower before sunrise. I don't know who the model was for you, but you are gorgeous. Not that I'm into girls, understand, but I can appreciate what my eyes tell me."

I'm not sure what I was thinking, talking to an image like that, but they were so real looking. It was just amazing. I dried and dressed and went out to join Misty and Princess. They were sitting on the bed with their eyes riveted on the tableau playing out before them.

"Come on, you two. You've got to see the dining room. There's even a band playing. It might be a limited menu, though. I'm not sure if the girl usually cooks real meals," I said, leading them to the door.

"Did you see what they're doing over there?" Misty asked. "They're undressing. I think they're going to, like, screw or something."

"Oh, don't worry. I'm sure they'll replay it if you miss anything fun."

"Why are you so calm about all this?" Princess asked. "There are ghosts everywhere!"

"That's what's so neat. Just look at the detail. Head to foot! Disney does a lot of eye direction. You get so caught up in a face that you don't really notice that there's nothing there below the shoulders. I tell you, the person who created all this is a genius!"

"You mean it doesn't bother you?" Princess asked.

"No. As soon as I figured out how to tell the real from the projections, it was all cool."

"How do you tell?"

"Watch the animals. When we went to the desk, they were sniffing at the clerk all over. They completely ignore the ghosts. I assume there are cast members circulating in the scene to make it more realistic." We entered the dining room.

"Warrior Wizard, it is a pleasure to welcome you to the banquet of the spirits. Please accompany me to your table." We followed him as I continued to lecture Princess and Misty.

"See? Like this guy," I said as I took hold of his shoulder, "is real and solid." Roadkill stuck his nose up the guy's butt and he involuntarily jerked.

"We're so glad you are enjoying the show. We seldom have any living beings here with us," the maître d' said. "We've taken the liberty of ordering our house specialty for you."

"As long as it's not brains and guts, I'm fine with that. But don't try to take advantage of us. That just won't work."

"Of course, Warrior Wizard." He turned left, intent on maintaining the illusion of a busy dining room. However, when it came time to serve the food, he was the one who brought the tray and the girl from the desk, dressed as a chef now, set the dishes on the table. I held up my hand to stop Misty and Princess from diving in. Instead, I quickly flipped the gold cord over the maître d' and pulled him to me.

"Now, kind sir," I said standing. "I'd ask you to please place your hand on the pommel of my sword."

"Yes, Warrior Wizard," he said, obeying my command.

"In this crazy world we live in, we can't be too careful. You know, I had to fight werewolves last night. So, I just want you to tell me precisely what is being served in our dinner and to affirm that it is safe to eat."

"Really," he sniffed. "We don't poison our guests. This is a rustic lamb fricassee with tender chunks of lamb, greens, artichokes and a delicious Greek avgolemono sauce. It is served over a bed of mixed wild rice. My daughter is exceptionally proud of her cooking ability."

"And you both have my sincere apologies for the doubt I cast. You just would not believe the week we've had. I do hope I'll have a chance to talk to you again. I just love what you've done with the place."

"Certainly, Warrior Wizard." I released the cord of submission and he let go of my sword of truth. I sat and we dug into one of the most exquisite dishes I've ever eaten. Princess and Misty ate enthusiastically, if a little more distracted by all the characters around us. I was trying to figure out if any of the musicians were actors or if they were all projections. The music certainly seemed to be coming from the stage.

And that's another thing that was different. We could hear voices from the other tables, but it was difficult to decide which table they came from. It was almost as if the sounds in the room were piped in. That had to be it. The maître d' brought us a nice baklava and coffee for dessert.

"Please sit with us and tell us more about your whole setup," I invited. He took a chair and everyone in the room seemed to turn to look at us.

"What can I tell you, Warrior Wizard? The story is long."

"But this is such a wonderful place, it must be worth the story. Please, indulge us."

"Very well. It started several years ago. An epidemic swept through the community and in a matter of a few weeks, we'd lost a third of our population to it," he said. "Another third pulled up stakes and left, abandoning their homes and everything in them. Of the remaining third, nearly half have passed on in the intervening years and there have been no new arrivals."

"How sad!"

"Yes. There are fewer than a hundred living souls in the town now. We were, frankly, devastated. None of us here have escaped unscathed, but all have lost people near and dear to them." The desk clerk, still dressed as a chef, pulled a chair to our table, seeming to be as hungry for conversation as the man. "Most of the people in the community were related in some way—if you went back far enough—so, the losses cut deeply, emotionally and physically. This, by the way, is my daughter Joan. I'm Raymond."

"Happy to meet you, Raymond. I'm Jackie. This is Princess and Misty. Joan, that was absolutely one of the best meals I have ever had. I hope you have enough business to merit your talents."

"Thank you. There aren't that many living people here to cook for, but I usually get a good meal in at least once a week," she said. I automatically transposed what she said to mean 'that many people living here.' I was sure that was what she meant.

"Sorrow and loss will drive people to do things we wouldn't have thought of otherwise. There weren't enough of us left to support the businesses, and we had to close many of them that no longer had living owners. We were talking—those of us who were left—one Sunday after church, about what a ghost town we were living in. One thing led to another, and what you see is the result."

It was an amazing story and I kept looking around for the gimmicks. Really hard to spot.

"Your engineer must be brilliant. This is the best I've ever seen. I have to ask, where are the projectors?" I said. He got a really puzzled look on his face and then a dawning of something. He reached over and took hold of my sword.

"I tell you this truthfully," he said. "These are not projections. They are the ghosts of the people we lost."

MAYBE—JUST MAYBE—HE COULD have surprised me more. I looked around the room and half a dozen people, obviously those among the living, had scooted their chairs closer to our table. Around them, the ghostly visages stood, grinning and waiting to see if I'd panic. There was a high-pitched whine and I looked first at Roadkill. He was fine. The whine was coming from Misty and Princess. Joan reached out and patted their shoulders. I'm not sure that comforted them.

"So, you're...?"

"A necromancer," he said. "Only I don't do animating dead bodies. There is nothing a sorcerer can do to stop the deterioration of the flesh. But the spirits of our friends are here and lively, happy to have a chance to get together for a party when we have a guest. We try to make it an interesting show."

"Oh, definitely," I laughed, much to Misty and Princess's amazement. "The woman in our bathtub was certainly putting on a show, and I think the couple in the reflected room were getting ready to do something pornographic."

"They do tend to enjoy exhibitionism," he said. "Nothing they ever would have done in life, but now there is nothing to stop them."

"How many guests do you get each day?"

"Each day?" Joan huffed. "We're lucky to see a living human stop in town once in a month."

"Oh no! How do you keep operating?" I said.

"I'm afraid it is a labor of love," Raymond said. "This way, at least I get to see my loving Cassandra, Joan's mother, once in a while." A woman walked up behind him and put a hand on his shoulder.

"Hi, Mom," Joan said. "Nice guests, aren't they?"

Raymond turned to see the woman behind him and they smiled at each other. It must be difficult to be able to see each other, but not to feel or hear.

"Is everyone here willingly?" I asked.

"Oh, yes. We called a big town meeting with my first summoning. Some bowed out and indicated they didn't want to participate. Those who gather are the ones who weren't ready to leave," Raymond said.

"We need to get you more guests!" I said with determination. "You just can't imagine what a demand there is for a good haunted house. And to have an entire haunted town? You could be making a fortune!"

"How?" asked one of the men seated near us. "We're just people who like to dress up and spend time with our friends and family."

"A little marketing," I said. "Now this is all if you're interested. I don't want to tell you how to run your lives. Or deaths, as the case may be. If you wanted to really entertain people, you could start by running an ad in some of the big newspapers. Radio and television, too. Don't limit yourselves to people nearby. You have a nice hotel, great meals, and a unique form of entertainment. How often does a person get to actually walk among the dead?"

"You think people would come here for that?" a woman asked.

"Oh, yeah. No question. Position it as a destination resort. Even invite people to bring their own ghosts. Not that I think there are a lot of necromancers out there who are raising people, but it will give people a big thrill to have dinner with an actual ghost. And if those three in our room keep putting on the show they are, it will be a special that's worth a premium," I said. I was getting excited and by the looks of them, the ghosts gathered around were, too.

"Do you really think this would work?" Raymond asked.

"You wouldn't believe the appetite people have for the macabre. All I'd say is that all of the performers need to be in agreement. You'd get a lot of bad press if they thought you were somehow forcing the dead to perform for you," I said.

"I think this could work!" Raymond said. "Joan could get more culinary skills in and the guests could have dinner with a ghost!"

"Now you're thinking. This place is a prime location. You even have a lake near and can have a beach open in the summer. Oh! And get some smells. If you have a hundred living people in town, someone could learn to run the espresso machine. Someone could bake a little something, even if it isn't much. And put a fan in the kitchen that blows the smell of what Joan is cooking up here. The first thing that clued me in that something was out of kilter was that I couldn't smell anything."

"Yes. We could do that."

"I'll even give you an endorsement," I said. "'Jackie the Warrior Wizard said to eat here, sleep here, and take a look at the other side.' We can rework that so it makes the most sense."

THE WHOLE TOWN got excited and brainstormed various attractions they could have. It was fun to have everyone vote in an impromptu poll. I watched.

"Abe, you can't keep voting," Joan said, chiding a ghost that was in line for the third time. "I can recognize you even when you change hats. Your vote has been recorded. The dead can vote here, but only once." Two other ghosts approached and escorted Abe out of the line. I saw the babe in the bathtub in line to vote. She'd put on a robe.

"Who is that?" I asked Raymond.

"Oh, that's Reba. Whenever we put a guest in that room, she rushes up there to get in the tub. Did you see her there?"

"Yeah. We had a nice shower together. I think she was just hoping I'd turn the shower on. She seemed to really like it," I said. "And she's damn cute!"

"I'll make a note of that and ask her about what she wants to do in terms of performing. She was always a bit of an exhibitionist. But she might not want guys perving on her. I can imagine some of them being pretty gross."

"If they're guys, that's a given," I sighed. "Well, I'm taking my crew and heading for bed. We need to get on the road at a decent hour tomorrow. We *do* have a quest to attend to."

"Thank you for all your help, Warrior Wizard. We'll have breakfast for you before you leave."

"ARE YOU SERIOUS?" Princess asked in shock. "You are going to tell people to come and dine with the ghosts? What if they hurt someone?"

"What would they do? They are apparitions. Intelligent apparitions who love their town and want to help it recover," I said.

"What if they start eating people?" Misty asked.

"Auntie, they are ghosts, not zombies. Now, it's close to midnight. We need to get moving in the morning. Let's go to bed."

I got in bed and went to sleep pretty quickly. Misty snuggled up and I felt her breathing change as she dropped off to sleep. I think Princess might have watched the late show with the couple in the mirror. She looked pretty exhausted in the morning.

I KEPT MY word and got up before sunrise to take a shower. Reba was waiting for me. When I started the water, she slipped out of her robe and joined me in the shower. It was a strange thing to look at her as the water sprayed through her. She faced it, shook her head in it, raised her hands to dance in it.

"Hey, don't slip and fall," I laughed. She just shrugged and raised up an inch or two off the tub surface. I guess the idea of slipping and falling didn't affect a ghost. "You love the shower, don't you?" I asked. She nodded emphatically. "But you can't really feel it, can you?" She sadly shook her head. Here she was, standing in the shower, loving every minute of it, but unable to actually feel it. It was really sad. "If I could make you materialize, for just a minute, do you think you could feel the water? I think I could do it, if you want me to. Nothing without your permission."

Reba was nodding her head so emphatically, I thought it would fall off. That would be unpleasant. I held up my hands and she held still. I placed my hands on either side of her head and visualized her becoming physically present. Then I muttered the words. "Se concrétiser."

I had my eyes closed, so the first clue I had was a gasp. I opened my eyes to see Reba with her face upturned to the warm water, arms held out, and a smile on her face. She opened her eyes and rushed to embrace me. I just held her in my arms for the few moments left before sunrise. I could feel her body losing its solidity as she slipped back into the nothingness of daytime.

"Thank you," I heard her whisper as the last vestige of her physical body evaporated.

I'd had my doubts about the whole process. I hoped the dissolving physical body didn't cause pain for her. And I really hoped that the moments of feeling the water on her body didn't make not having it more difficult for her.

"Blessings on you, Reba. Blessings," I whispered. I turned the water off and got out of the shower. It was time to face another day.

MILE 1308

"WATCH FOR A turn off to the left," Misty said. "It should be coming up in just... right now!"

I saw the turnoff as we sped by it. I wished the damn TripTik would give us a little more warning on things. We'd almost missed the café half an hour ago. I screeched to a stop and we got the animals out for a walk. Also managed to get a fresh cup of pretty good coffee. Now the TripTik wants me to turn immediately. I slowed to a stop after checking the mirrors to make sure there was nothing behind us. We hadn't had much traffic, but the road wasn't deserted either. I put the car in reverse and backed up until I'd reached the side road and turned.

For most of this journey, we'd been traveling on a good quality blacktop, two-lane road with a wide shoulder on either side. The road we turned onto was a narrow two-lane byway that could use some repairs. In some places, there was a ditch that dropped off beside the road. A little nudge to the right and the tire would drop down into the ditch and we'd break an axle, among other things. We started gaining elevation at once.

And the road got worse.

"Are you sure this is the way?" I asked. I'd never really looked at the TripTik and simply trusted that Misty was giving me good directions. The road turned to gravel.

"The route is clearly marked, but there are some pretty tight curves coming up," she said.

"Look over there!" Princess said pointing out the passenger side window. I couldn't see. Misty looked out her window.

"Better slow down and take a look at this," she said.

I slowed to a stop again, but I couldn't see what they were fascinated by, so I got out and walked around to the back. "Misty, bring the binoculars, please," I said. She brought the glasses from the glovebox and I looked down the mountain to the road we'd left behind. What Princess had spotted was a roadblock of the highway we'd been following. Lots of heavy machinery was blocking the way. What she couldn't see, however, was the number of men running around in black suits. One of them was identifiable: Valentine Caesar. How the heck did he get ahead of us?

It would be helpful to have a larger detailed map so we could tell where we were going and how far it would be. All we had was the not-to-scale map of the Land that showed general relationships of major landmarks, and the TripTik that showed what was immediately in front of us. It had just saved us from running smack into the enemy.

We all piled back into the car and kept going, though I went at a bit slower pace so as not to raise much dust that might be visible from the highway. Before long, I didn't need to worry about that either. The gravel road changed to a track barely wide enough for the car to get through. I kept driving around the curves and finally realized we were headed back downhill instead of heading for the summit.

We'd shifted and it looked like we'd crossed a shoulder of the mountain and were headed down the other side. As the track became wider and then became dirt and gravel, I managed to gradually accelerate. It was still a long haul and we made several rest stops along the way to relieve bladders and grab food and drinks from the unending supply in the back of the hatch. Eventually, we hit a main road again. I had no idea if it was the same main road. It's not like any of the routes were marked with names or anything. It was just 'go this way' or 'turn here.'

When the TripTik pointed us to another campground, I was suspicious, but this was a small place with just a couple other campers in it. We didn't have a typically reserved spot, but found a space sort of secluded. We were all so tired that we set up camp, ate, and slept.

Chapter 11

Here There Be Dragons

IT WAS DOWNRIGHT SPOOKY in the morning to just wake up, fix breakfast, and break camp without any conflicts, attacks, strange people, or weirdness around us. The other campers were also stirring, but each allowing the others their privacy. It looked like a family camp and most of the people were there for longer than a single night.

As we sat around our fire eating breakfast and drinking coffee, we saw people out walking—some looking like they were prepared for a major hike. We returned their waves and everyone smiled. I started getting uneasy. This was just too idyllic. Then a couple stopped and turned in at our campsite with their friendly wave.

"Welcome, strangers," the man said. "We're the camp hosts, Frankie and Johnnie. You planning to stay on a while?"

"Oh, no," I drawled. "We're just overnighting. Do we owe a fee?"

"The campgrounds in Victoriana are free to the public. No fees necessary," the woman responded. "You must be on a quest. Do you need any information?"

"As a matter of fact," Misty said, "we're looking for Baron Federico Rex, who was kidnapped from East Love."

"Oh! Didn't know he'd been kidnapped. Old man Hakuryū said the boy was his great nephew. If you just continue up this road—oh, I'd say—thirty miles, you'll get to Gold Bar. Pretty good sized city for this part of the Land," the man said. "Turn left at—let me see now, one, two, yeah—the third traffic light, and just outside the city limits you'll come to The Trove. It's a gated community where everyone is rich, beautiful, and pleasant. Two out of three. I'm not exactly sure which place is Hakuryū's, but someone there should be able to tell you."

"You mean everyone knows this Hakuryū and that he has the Sovereign's son in his house and no one has done anything about it?" I asked in disbelief.

"Well, the boy—Baron—is kind of a local legend. He's got the best Last Battle score going and is an absolute wizard at the Quazar Arcade."

"Ha!" Princess exploded. "I can beat him at Last Battle anytime."

"Let's not start the negotiations with a challenge," I said. "Remember you have a different goal. Maybe he's gotten better."

"Yeah. Like, sure."

"I think we should pack up and hit the road. Looks like we're near our goal," Misty said. I thanked the camp hosts and we got the tent and food put away. I doused the coals while Roadkill and Shasta took one more outdoor opportunity and the rest of us used the latrines again. It was definitely time to move.

MILE 1364

THE TRIPTIK AGREED with the host's directions and in a little over an hour, we were pulling up to the gated community, The Trove. What a strange name. I gave the gate attendant the name of Hakuryū and that the Wizard Warrior and Princess were calling. I wanted to include Misty, too, but she didn't have a title, so I just said, 'and company.' It seemed to be adequate for the guard. He called someone and then opened the gate.

"Last one, straight ahead," he said, waving us through. It was almost as if we were expected. I wondered if Valentine got here before us.

The community was entirely huge estates with a hodgepodge of every style dwelling imaginable, as long as the McMansion could be supersized. There was a soaring glass contemporary next to a Victorian gingerbread. Then one made of stone and another in typical Texas-style colonial with a two-story entry and columns along the front. The last house on the cul-de-sac was a Gothic mansion straight out of Frankenstein. Oh, that was a comforting thought!

We drove straight up to the parking area in front of the doors and all jumped out of the car. I was looking around for possible threats, but didn't even see another car. I assumed they must be inside the carriage house. I laughed at that, because there was a basketball hoop above one of the garage doors. Well, maybe Baron was the active type. The door of the mansion opened and a man in a butler outfit—I guess it's just a tux with tails and white gloves—stepped out to greet us.

"Please come in and refresh yourselves. Mister Hakuryū begs your pardon until the mid-day repast as he is terribly busy at the moment. I have prepared a room for you. Please forgive me if my assumption that you would all want to room together is incorrect."

"A room?" I said. "I suppose it wouldn't hurt to freshen up. We camped out last night. Okay. Thanks." He led us up a massive flight of stairs and along a second floor balcony to double doors that opened into a light and airy room with a huge bed on one side and correctly sized dog and cat beds at the foot. He pointed at a bell cord.

"If you need anything at all, just ring." He bowed and pulled the doors closed behind him.

"This place is bigger than the ghost hotel," Princess said.

"How did that butler guy know we were going to arrive today so he had a room ready for us?" Misty asked. "And how did he know how many and of what species are in our party? Look, a dog and cat bed just the right size."

"Yeah. Look in the bathroom," Princess added. "Three sets of towels, fluffy robes, and even our favorite shampoos."

"It seems strange," I said, "but everything that happens seems strange to me these days. If Mr. Hakuryū is busy 'until mid-day repast,' why didn't he take us to see Baron? And why am I so tired, I think I'll pass out on that big bed?"

"Do we dare?" Misty asked, bouncing on the side of the bed.

"We're in the dragon's lair now. It's too late to question his hospitality," I yawned. We all three collapsed and went to sleep.

THE KNOCKING ON the door woke us up. I jumped out of bed to find out what was going on.

"Dinner will be served in forty-five minutes. Your clothes have been cleaned and pressed. There are fresh towels in the bath. Please follow Midge to the dining room when you are ready," the butler said when I opened the door.

"Okay. Sure." I looked behind him and a small woman nodded and bobbed her head. I turned back to my companions. Misty and Princess jumped out of bed naked and I realized I was bare as well.

"When did they take our clothes?" Princess asked. "I don't remember undressing."

"There are only three possibilities," Misty pronounced as she headed toward the shower. "Either we got up and took them off so they could be cleaned and then forgot about it; or we were so deeply asleep that they came in and undressed us without waking us up; or the clothes were spirited off our bodies and cleaned by magic." She paused in the doorway while I spoke.

"Or four: Jackie is dreaming and that detail wasn't important, so it was skipped over."

"Yeah. Or that," Misty said. She started the shower and we cycled in and out, getting ourselves dressed in clothes that looked as good as new. There wasn't a speck of blood on any of my clothes, which I found amazing after the amount that had been sprayed on me. When Midge rapped softly on our door, we were ready. Even the dog and cat had clean vests and boots and collars. It was like being in the last scene of *Star Wars* where they all go into the award ceremony sparkling clean in the same clothing they did battle in. Did it ever strike you as strange that the only person in that entire series who ever changed clothes was Princess Leia? We followed Midge to the dining room.

Mr. Hakuryū greeted us. Standing beside him was ten-year-old Baron Federico Rex.

"Rico!" Princess said, jumping forward to hug her brother.

"Bridge," he answered, embarrassed by the outpouring but still wanting to hug his sister.

"My gosh, you've grown! You're almost as tall as I am," Princess said.

"Yeah, but you've always been short," he answered.

"Come, children. Heroes. Familiars. Let's sit and relate adventures as we eat." He seated Baron next to him and Princess to the seat beside her brother. The butler ushered me to the other side of Hakuryū and Misty sat beside me. The dog and cat had places on the floor at the foot of the table. The food began arriving in abundance! I didn't realize how hungry I'd become. It seemed like every time I turned around, I was hungry again.

"You wouldn't believe the game room here!" Baron was telling his sister. "Ryu and I spend hours a day there. We were in a huge contest this morning that went on until about an hour ago."

"What were you playing?"

"Last Battle. It was epic!"

"Think you can beat me at it?" Princess challenged.

"Oh, yeah. No sweat. I've studied all your moves," Baron said.

"Why did you study all her moves?" I asked. "Sounds like some pretty serious research."

"Ryu says a good warrior studies the moves of his enemy so he can see the weaknesses. It's also so that when something surprises you, you can quickly identify that it is new and categorize it. You aren't surprised by every move," Baron said. He was talking like a general.

"So, you just play games here all the time?" Misty asked. "Baron hasn't gone to school in the past year?"

"School. Ick!" Baron said succinctly.

"Perhaps so, but it is necessary," Hakuryū said. "We have tutors who come nearly every day. I assure you I have not neglected young Baron's education."

"I guess we should talk about why we're here," I said. "We need to take Baron back to East Love for the succession celebration."

"I don't wanna go," the boy said. I winced.

"I would miss him terribly if he left," Hakuryū said. "Perhaps if I send some kind of gift to his parents, they will consent to let him stay."

"I have to say that everything seems fine here, but there are other things to consider. If Baron does not appear, there will be a general election for a successor. The most likely candidate is Valentine Caesar. I assume you know him from having him bring Baron here," I said.

"In fact, I chased him off and refused to have him visit again," Hakuryū said. "A thoroughly disgusting young man."

"At least our opinion of him matches. He's been trying to stop us from getting here every step along the way. As if there weren't enough natural dangers," I said. "His grandfather has apparently been importing and strong-arming people in East Love and perhaps all over the Land to vote for Valentine as a replacement. If Valentine is elected as successor, he will sue for Princess Bridget Rex's hand in marriage to cement the position. We really want to avoid that."

"I'd have to wait a year before I could poison him and inherit the succession," Princess said. "You should be glad you aren't a girl, Baron. Nobody listens to what you want."

"Nobody listens to me, either, except Ryu."

"August Caesar is a wizard of some power," Ryu said. "That's the only reason I've kept Baron here. I didn't think it was safe to send him home."

"Maybe there's a way to make everyone happy," Misty volunteered. We all turned our attention to her as she fed some chicken from her plate to Shasta. "Baron, you have a place here with Hakuryū that you don't want to leave. I don't blame you at all. Mr. Hakuryū wants you to stay. Princess wants to be the successor to her father and rule all the Land. I'm all for that. She'll make a wonderful Sovereign. But we have the problem of the interloper and the succession celebration, which could dash everyone's dreams. Why don't you come back to East Love for the celebration, then abdicate in favor of your sister? Then you can come back here with Mr. Hakuryū, if he really wants you. How does that sound?"

"I wouldn't have to go back and live there forever? Ryu, could I really come back here?"

"I would be delighted to have you back, son. I believe Miss Misty has presented a plan that is acceptable to all of us. And I believe I can make it acceptable to your parents," the old man said. "It is not uncommon for royalty to give a hostage as a sign of goodwill to powerful lords in the land. I will press ancient treaty rights. There are not many of my kind left in the Land, but we could create an enormous amount of trouble if upset."

"Your kind?" I asked. I wondered if he meant Japanese.

"I am descended from the ancient dragon of Japan, Ryujin. The bloodline has been thinned through inter-marriage over the years, but many peoples in the southern part of the Land of Victoriana owe their allegiance to me."

"We actually *are* in the dragon's lair," I sighed. "I suppose you controlled our sleep this afternoon and had our clothes cleaned."

"That was a liberty I took," the dragon said. "I assure you, however, that none of you will age a hundred years in a night here in The Trove."

"The association seems to be to our benefit and to the benefit of Baron and Princess. I'm pleased to not need to fight for his release," I said.

"As to that, there might be a small problem," Hakuryū said. I raised an eyebrow. "You see, once having arrived here in The Trove, you might find it difficult to leave. Since Valentine brought Baron to me, he has convinced a giant named Fum that I have family heirlooms that rightly belong to the giant. Fum has been harrying us for months, attempting to get into the mansion and lay waste to all around us."

"And with all your power, you have been unable to get rid of him?"

"As many people do, you confuse wealth with power," he answered. "Wealth seems not to interest Fum and I can identify nothing in my collections that might remotely belong to him or his family."

"So, I've got to do battle with him before we can take Baron back to East Love. Great. Just great," I moaned. I was really tired of fighting people or things or creatures. I'd been so relieved when I discovered I wouldn't need to slay the dragon in order to take Baron. A giant didn't sound fun either. But that wasn't all.

"I'll go on one condition," Baron said.

"Wait a minute! I thought your condition was being able to come back," I said. "What's with new conditions?"

"Bridget thinks she can take me in Last Battle. We'll play a match this afternoon while you're waiting for Fum to show up. If she can beat me, I'll go back home and abdicate in her favor. If she can't beat me, she isn't worthy of becoming sovereign. I'll stay here and she can marry Valentine," the boy declared.

That came right out of left field. I didn't think it was a good idea for several reasons. First, he'd been practicing non-stop for nearly a year. I didn't know how much practice Princess had over that time, but I felt like she'd be better off facing the giant. Second, if she lost, I'd end up having to fight the giant and the dragon in order to take the brat home. After all, that was my quest. And finally… I didn't get to express my opinions.

"You're on, twerp. I can beat you at Last Battle any time," Princess declared. She stuck out her hand and Baron grabbed it to shake on the deal. I groaned, and dragged Princess with me out of the room.

"Do you realize what you've done?" I barked at her. "If you don't beat him, you forfeit your chance at the throne. Not only that, but I still have to drag his ass with me, which means I'll have to fight both the giant *and* the dragon. You make my job difficult and your goal impossible!"

"Don't worry, Warrior Wizard. He said he's been studying my play. That can work for him or against him. It would work for him if what he studied was still my play. It works against him when he realizes I'm not the same as the person he's been studying," Princess said.

"What do you mean?"

"I changed my online identity and avatar over a year ago without telling him. Besides, his focus is just on winning. My focus is on the prize. The prize doesn't mean anything to him. It isn't a motivator. There is nothing in his conditions that in any way helps him. All he wants to do is win and he doesn't lose a thing if he loses."

"I still don't like it."

"You just take care of the giant. I'll take care of the brat."

I DON'T KNOW if you've watched a multi-player RPG online or not. It's boring! Nobody does anything but sit there and roll their dice and announce their moves. Mr. Hakuryū was the game master and I had no question that he would be fair. He seemed like a reasonable man… or dragon… and had nothing to gain by playing favorites. After an eternity that took at least an hour, I excused myself from the game room and went outside.

It was early evening and with mountains to the west of us, the sun was nearing the point at which it would disappear. It's just never a good idea to leave me with nothing to do. I went to the Fairlane and grabbed my basketball and court shoes out of the hatch. I changed shoes and started to dribble. I already had my slingshot holstered on my belt. I wasn't going to get my gun out of the car. There's something different about drawing a bead and shooting a werewolf and drawing a bead and shooting a man—even if it is a giant man. I couldn't help but think it was human. Probably a deadly weakness in my preparation to do battle.

I dribbled over and started shooting hoops. I still couldn't figure out how the ball had become a flaming missile when I threw it at Valentine's men, but just handled like a normal basketball when I started dribbling. I did my usual warmups, and then started popping baskets, doing dribbling drills, and shooting around the world. It felt good. Basketball season had ended over two months ago and all I did was run hurdles during track season.

As I dribbled toward the garage and basket, I was struck by the echo. It was like a bounce for every dribble

I made, coming from behind me. I turned, and there he was. *Oh, damn!*

He had me in height by a good foot and some inches. Off hand, I'd say he was about seven-and-a-half feet tall. But that wasn't the problem. If you've read any illustrated fairy tales with giants in them, you know they are huge ugly oafs. Some have two heads. They always have a beard and hair that's black and sticks out in all directions. They have missing or rotted teeth and rags for clothes. And they're dumb as a post. The very name Fum was reminiscent of the giant who went about yelling, "Fee-fi-fo-fum, I smell the blood of an Englishman." Even Hagrid was portrayed as being a simple burly giant of a man with a coarse black beard and hair, barrel-chested, and ham-fisted. He got along with animals better than with people.

Not so, the giant that was approaching, dribbling a basketball in counterpoint to mine. No. Better think Chris Hemsworth as Thor or Brad Pitt as Achilles or Kellan Lutz as Hercules. I was facing a blond god out of ancient mythology or off the pages of Marvel Comics. I was not prepared for this!

"So, you're my nemesis," he said. Oh, what rich lovely tones. His voice was as beautiful as he was. "Shall we get warmed up?" Warmed up? I'd started to warm up as soon as I saw him! I just nodded and he launched his ball at the hoop. Swish, of course. He cleared the ball and glanced at me as I took my shot from behind the three-point line and drained it. We each took shots and recovered our own basketball. We switched from long shots to layups, each watching the other's skill and technique. I had a feeling that someplace along the line, we were going to go at each other, but it was just too nice to watch him to want to attack. In that way.

He was wearing a cut-off basketball jersey and a pair of shorts. When he jumped for a shot, the shirt rode up farther and showed off his unbelievable abs. They complemented his well-defined arms and muscular legs. Our shots came faster and faster. And then there was the dunk. He could practically reach over the rim of the basket standing flat-footed. A little hop and he slammed it home. Well, I had to jump a little harder, but I wasn't going to be left behind. I took a step and dunked my own. He turned to me, tucked his ball under his arm, and applauded. God! The smile on his face was killer.

"One-on-one?" he asked. I nodded. "Are you really going to play in robes, Warrior Wizard?"

I must have looked ridiculous. I still had my cap and gown on with all my regalia. I had the sword of truth and the slingshot on my belt. My three cords and stole were around my neck. I grinned at him. Somehow, I didn't feel exactly threatened, but I was really excited. I tossed my mortarboard in the open hatch of the car and unzipped my gown. I shrugged it off my shoulders and tossed it in the car as well. I got a lot more excited when he gave a low whistle.

Well, we practiced in sports bras and court shorts all the time. It wasn't a basketball uniform, but it left us free to move and work up a sweat. And I could tell this was going to get sweaty.

Now, the rules of one-on-one. Offensive player stands outside the half-court line, which in this case was the edge of the paved court. Defensive player passes the ball to the offensive player and it's game on. There's a lot of dribbling in this game because if you stop dribbling, you have to shoot without traveling. So, you use every dribbling trick you can to get clear for your shot. Through the legs. Behind the back. Between your opponent's legs. Any way you can confuse him before you break free for your shot. If you hit it, you have a point and continued possession of the ball. If you miss, sides change and you pass the ball to your opponent who is now on offense.

Adonis, as I'd come to think of him, passed me the ball and I started working it forward. That was a lot of man to try to get around. But it was obvious he was used to playing against opponents who tried to shoot over him or were as tall as he was. He didn't crouch low, but stood to block the shot from wherever you took it. I think he was genuinely surprised when I dribbled around him and shot from under the basket. I wouldn't get that easy a point again. He grinned at me and passed me the ball again. I was right. He stayed with me wherever I tried to move. When I finally shot, he jumped halfway across the court to block it before it reached the hoop.

His ball. He dribbled forward with a couple of feints and jumped for the shot. I think he was genuinely shocked to find he no longer had the ball in his hands. I was below his radar and as soon as he went for the shot, I grabbed the ball away and dribbled to the backcourt. My ball. Score still one to nothing.

And then it heated up. I'm sure what we were doing was more thrilling than what Baron and Princess were up to in the game room, but it's still tedious to deliver a play-by-play. You really needed to be there, getting hotter and sweatier by the minute. And as we got more aggressive, we got into each other's personal space a lot more. And before long, his shirt was lying by the garage door and we were sliding off each other as we went for our shots.

It was full dark before we even thought about slacking off. Mr. Hakuryū had lights that came on as the daylight failed. We dribbled, shot, blocked, recovered, and dribbled some more. I gradually became aware of his hand on me. That's not unusual when you're playing ball. Placing a hand lightly in contact with your opponent is one way of cluing in on which direction he or she is headed. It's not considered a foul. A lot of offensive players back toward their opponent, keeping the ball in front of them and out of reach. So, the defense keeps a hand lightly on the waist or back of the offense. In one-on-one, that doesn't really work. It puts the offensive player at a disadvantage when it comes to knowing where the defense is going.

So, he seemed to also have a hand on my shoulder or hip. It was like dancing. And I responded the same way. Was the hand meant to keep a distance between us or to draw us closer? I just knew that we were playing my favorite game and I *really* liked the way we played it.

He shook free and started the steps that would take him to a slam dunk. I don't know what got into me, but I leapt as he leapt. I was going for the block, I thought. I grabbed the ball, but his momentum pulled me upward several inches as he jumped for the basket. I wrapped my legs around his waist. I still had my hands on the ball, but more importantly, my eyes met his. Then my lips met his. Then the basketball just fell to the ground and bounced away as our arms wrapped around each other.

Chapter 12

Giant-Size Crush

I WOKE UP in the morning, wrapped in the arms of my Greek god. We never made it into the house. Mr. Hakuryū's lawn was soft and well-manicured and my graduation gown made a fine bed. Roadkill sprawled across us made a blanket. Fum woke up and looked into my eyes with a big smile.

"I suppose you want something I'm not supposed to give," he sighed. We'd already had most everything. It took me a minute to figure out what else I might want. Then I remembered.

"Oh. Yeah. I suppose so. I'm supposed to take Baron Federico Rex to his parents' home in East Love. But then if everything goes well, we're bringing him right back here," I said, hoping that would ease the conflict. "Don't you think that would count? You could go right back to guarding him."

"You have slain me, Warrior Wizard Jackie. I am yours to do with as you wish. Not only will I let you go, I'll escort you to see you safely there," he said, kissing me again. So dreamy.

"Maybe I can get Misty and Princess to ride with Mr. Hakuryū and the two of us can ride together," I said.

"Mmm. Nice car, but I don't think I'll fit. I'll follow in mine." He pointed toward the opposite side of the drive where a utilitarian white Ford Super Duty F250 was parked.

"I bet you can keep up with me," I grinned. "Let's go in and have some breakfast. I'm starving."

"I don't know. I might not be welcome there. He's got a family heirloom of mine and we've been a little in conflict over it."

"Neither of you is going to be anything but nice and polite as long as I'm there. Besides, I might have to fight Mr. Hakuryū to take Baron with me if he won the game against his sister last night."

"I hope not, because I could not stand to see you in danger. I don't think he plays basketball," Fum said.

"How did you get the name Fum? It seems so undignified. You are certainly a man with dignity," I said.

"My baby sister," he said. I raised an eyebrow at him. "My name is actually Freedom. When Libby was little, she couldn't get the whole word out. I became Fum and it's stuck with me ever since."

"Freedom is a wonderful name. Do you mind if I use that?"

"I'd be delighted if you used my real name, Jackie. I'd like to hear it from your lips over and over."

"Take it, Freedom. Take it from my lips." I lifted my head so he could bend to my kiss. What an experience! Even the guys I went out with who were tall, weren't *tall* like this. I looked up to him and was smitten. We were on the steps at the door when the butler opened it and looked up at us. He twitched a little, but scarcely responded to the two of us standing together.

"Mr. Hakuryū invites you in for breakfast," he said, standing back with the door open. "Watch your heads."

The warning was pointless as the doors and halls in the mansion were easily ten feet high. I saw Freedom instinctively duck anyway. I suppose I did, too. We were led immediately to the dining room where Hakuryū, Misty, Princess, Baron, Roadkill, and Shasta were already seated. Interestingly, Princess now sat across from her brother instead of next to him. Misty was next to Princess. There were two seats at the end of the table set for Freedom and me. We nodded politely as we were seated.

"Mr. Hakuryū, Princess Bridget Rex, Baron Federico Rex, Misty, Roadkill, and Shasta," I said. "Please let me introduce you all to my boyfriend, Freedom."

"Boyfriend?" Misty squeaked. "He'll never fit! I mean, in the car!"

"It must have been a very interesting match," Hakuryū said.

"Oh, it was. I kind of lost track of the score, though."

"Warrior Wizard Jackie has slain the loneliness within me and I am bound to her with chains of love," he said reaching for my hand. I swooned. How poetic.

"How went the Last Battle indoors?" I asked. Baron stood at his seat and I thought he was going to claim victory, but apparently Hakuryū had schooled him well.

"There is but one person I will ever call Sovereign after my parents have retired from the field. That person has shown her ability to defeat me on the open field of battle with superb strategy and tactics. I will gladly abdicate my place on the throne in favor of my sister, Princess Bridget Rex, and intend to travel with you to East Love to establish the same. Hail to the Sovereign heir!" the boy said. Hakuryū nodded his approval. Princess stood and faced her brother.

"I have found the test to be rigorous and my brother to be a stalwart, worthy, and honorable opponent. Now, however, I offer my hand in peace across this table, accepting your homage but also recognizing your place in the Land. One day, my brother, you will be the general who commands the armies of Victoriana. Hail to the General!" She reached across the table and they shook hands. It was a Kodak moment. Too bad we had no paparazzi snapping pictures.

"It seems we have one more order of business and we can all go happily on our way," Hakuryū said. "Fum…"

"Freedom is his name," I broke in. Hakuryū looked at me, startled. He nodded and settled down again.

"Mr. Freedom, I have been accused of stealing certain undescribed family heirlooms of yours. I cannot let that claim go unsettled. I assure you I do not even *know* your family and could not have collected anything of theirs. I must demand an apology and putting to rest these claims," he said.

Great. I could still end up with a battle on my hands and I didn't want to think which of the men might win. Freedom had strength and mass on his side, along with a pretty good brain, as far as I could tell. Hakuryū had age, experience, and untested magic. He'd said he could use his powers against the giant, but that might only be true outside his house.

"My parents—both as tall as I am—were once performers in a circus sideshow," Freedom started. I saw Hakuryū crease his brow and shift uncomfortably.

"There's nothing to be ashamed of in that," he said. "Many people who were 'unusual' took jobs performing when they couldn't get work in any other line."

"I project no shame on my parents," Freedom said. "But the circus master was a hard man. I won't say cruel. No one was treated any better or worse than he was, but he held the line firmly and demanded unquestioned obedience. The circus prospered, but not so the performers. They were little more than slaves, unable to escape because they had nowhere to go. When they finally had an opportunity to escape, my parents left with nothing but the clothes on their back and fled into the wilderness. What little they owned, they left in their circus wagon."

"That's a sad story, Mr. Freedom. I'm still not sure how it relates to me," Hakuryū said.

"My mother had one treasure: a cameo given to her by a former lover that she wore all the time. I'm told my parents escaped because their wagon broke an axle. They watched for the driver to leave to get help and then rushed from the wagon. In the process, her cameo necklace was pulled off. It was left lying on the floor of the wagon. I have spent most of my adult life searching for their wagon and the lost cameo. It might seem a small thing to you, cameos are not typically valuable pieces of jewelry, but it was all my mother had from her lover. I wish to take it to her to give to my sister. I believe you came into possession of that wagon and as a result, the cameo within it. You see, you owned that circus."

We all sat silently and watched Mr. Hakuryū process the information. It was a startling and revealing story. Even believing no ill of him, it was easy to see how the precious family heirloom would have come into his possession.

"It has been many years since I owned a circus. I'm sure you were yet unborn when it was dismantled and everyone went away. If my circus was the one your parents were in—which is not entirely likely—I would probably not have your heirloom in my possession. Nor could you identify it, based on what you have said. We are still at an impasse," Hakuryū said. "How would I ever find such a thing among my possessions, let alone verify that it is the one you seek?"

"Even if I had not been told by the Caesars that you still had the entire circus wagons and equipment in your possession, I believe you know precisely what cameo I am referring to."

He pulled up the sleeve of his T-shirt and showed his well-muscled shoulder. I must say, I was willing to remove the entire shirt from him and then just keep going. But he turned his shoulder toward the table and we all see the elegant tattoo. I hadn't noticed it in the dark, when we were both... uh... showing a lot of skin. It was a woman facing us, wearing a locket around her neck. Wrapped around the woman so that nothing indecent was exposed, was a dragon.

"You see, Mr. Hakuryū, it was the only thing she was wearing the night you made love. This image was inked in my skin as a reminder that I should seek the dragon in possession of the cameo, for he is my true father."

There was a stunned silence. Baron scowled at Freedom because the boy thought he'd just taken the place of a son to Hakuryū. He was not interested in an interloper.

"That was such a long time ago," Hakuryū whispered.

"I'm twenty-six years old."

"Time is different for dragons. The morning after she was stolen away from me, I was a hundred years older than I'd been the night before. The broken axle was no accident, but was contrived by the other giant in the circus who had designs on her. Since that morning, I have been working my way back in time to find her. When I awoke, the circus wagons had all been abandoned long before. They were derelicts parked on this very spot. I converted them into my home and began searching for the treasures that have built this mansion. But all the time I was looking for the beautiful giantess, Rhianna—sworn to kill the oaf that took her away."

"He's already dead. Mother never told me exactly how he died, but just that he had a 'weak stomach.' I was six years old and my little sister was just a year. She renamed us Freedom and Liberty that day."

"I need... I want... I'm over nine hundred years old and I don't know what I should do," Hakuryū sighed.

"I have not come to make any claim upon you other than to return the cameo so my mother can hand it to my sister. It was my mother's only heirloom," Freedom said.

"You shall have it," Hakuryū declared, "when your mother places it in your hand. I will give it to no other than my precious Rhianna."

"Then I'll..."

"Wait!" I cried out. "Don't go making statements of bravado! Don't make threats! Don't speak in absolutes! Just stop it!" I was surprised when they both stopped where they were and turned to me. "Freedom, Mr. Hakuryū's proposal fulfills your quest as well. What difference does it make if he places the cameo in your mother's hand or if you do? Either way, she'll give it to your sister. Where does your mother live?"

"A long way south of here. In the land of Adavena."

"We need to make the trip north to East Love so we can restore order to the land of Victoriana. Then you and I and Mr. Hakuryū can turn south and find your mother to return the cameo." There was a soft growl beside me and I glanced down at Roadkill. "And Baron and Misty and Shasta and Roadkill," I said.

"Me, too," Princess said.

"We'll need a caravan," I sighed.

"Don't you have duties and responsibilities at the capital?" Misty asked Princess.

"Not really. Once the succession is set, all I need to do is show up each year on succession day. Speaking of which, you know it's only a few days away and this whole adventure will have been a waste if Valentine is the only one who shows up," Princess said. I rolled my eyes at Misty and she rolled hers right back at me.

"And you two," I said to Freedom and Hakuryū, "can use the time to get to know each other like a father and son." Both men scowled, but didn't say a thing.

"How far is it back to East Love?" Misty asked.

"We've traveled a thousand miles to get here," I sighed.

"It's only 450 miles from here to East Love," the butler said. "If we can get out of here by noon, we can camp overnight a few miles from the Solo Bridge. You could all pack what you need and get freshened up," he wrinkled his nose at Freedom and me, "while I get the carriages ready. We'll be at East Love late tomorrow."

"The celebration!" Hakuryū exclaimed. "There's no reason we shouldn't take *everyone*. We should all be there for the Succession Day Festival. Call up the entire company, Jeeves. Or what's left of them."

"If you will accompany me, I have prepared a room so you can freshen up while I get the wagons ready," the butler said to Freedom and me. "Please forgive me if I've overstepped. I assumed you might want a room for the two of you separate from the rest of your party," he whispered. Freedom and I both blushed but held hands as we entered the room the butler showed us.

THE CARAVAN THAT set out from The Trove just after noon was the strangest thing I'd ever seen. There were five huge circus wagons. Each was hitched behind a gaily painted pickup truck like a travel trailer.

"When I woke up from my nap, the wagons were terribly deteriorated, as I said," Hakuryū told us. "And they were completely out of date. I completely renovated and updated them, with better suspension and tires, electricity, water, sewer connections, a kitchen, and an awning to shade the entrance of each wagon. As I did the work, I happened onto performers I had known or who were children or grandchildren of performers I'd known. It turned out that we all clustered in this single neighborhood and only venture out on occasion, but we spend a lot of time in our wagons."

Hakuryū had his own wagon and truck. This made the adventure much more exciting for Baron than riding 450 miles in the back seat of a car with his sister and two animals. The butler and maid, Jeeves and Midge, were a couple and had their own truck and wagon. Jeeves made sure Freedom's truck was properly equipped and hooked up the giant's wagon to it. Freedom was over the moon happy to have his mother's circus wagon to pull. And up in the front of the caravan was my 1968 Ford Fairlane 500 Fastback. I checked around to be sure everyone was in. Misty, Princess, Roadkill, and Shasta. Behind me, Freedom smiled and waved. Then came Mr. Hakuryū and Baron, followed by Jeeves and Midge. I hadn't met the drivers of the last two wagons, which were bunkhouses. I was informed we'd be picking up other people along the way.

I started the Fairlane, raised my hand out the window, and waved the caravan forward. "Where to, Misty?" I asked. She happily opened the TripTik and pointed me to the left. The caravan followed.

MILE 1557

"WELL, DO YOU believe now? You've met werewolves, ghosts, and a dragon. And let us not forget the giant," Misty said as we drove along the highway. Princess and the animals were singing along with one of the country songs that seemed to be on every station we tuned the radio to.

"How can it be?" I sighed. "I must be dreaming. You know, they say you can dream a lifetime overnight. I'm afraid I'm going to wake up and Mr. Rogers will be calling my name to come and get the diploma before he throws it out. None of this can be real."

"Not even Freedom?"

I heaved a huge sigh. "I don't want to wake up. He's the best thing I've ever come across. We played hard and not like he was giving me points. We were well-matched on the court and then it got really physical, and talk about being well-matched. I was so afraid I was going to wake up when we went in to take a shower that I took him in with me. And you know... One thing led to another."

"Really?" she said sarcastically.

"Yeah. And another. I can hardly stand that he's in the truck behind me and not sitting beside me. Or maybe that I'm in the Fairlane instead of his truck. I just know I'm going to be heartbroken when I wake up. It's not fair."

"Of course, you could simply admit that it's all real and not have to worry about waking up," Misty said. "Would that be so bad?"

"I don't know. Would I end up with one quest after another until one of them kills me? I've already got enemies at Thunder Mountain among the snakes. And speaking of snakes, there's the Caesars. And then the border patrol at Anatnomia and the werewolves. What kind of stupid stuff would I have to do to complete the next quest?"

"Well, if the next quest was making sure a certain cameo got to a certain giant's mother, it might not be so bad," Misty chuckled.

"I personally object to being considered a dream," Princess said. "I have my own dreams and it just doesn't make sense to have my dreams be part of your dream of me dreaming. When you wake up, you're going to realize we were all real and you missed out by considering us all dreams."

"I'm sorry, Princess. I don't mean to imply you aren't real. It's me that isn't real. I'm using my dream state to visit your world. How does that sound?" I asked. I had an answer in my mind before she spoke.

"Lame."

"Yeah. It is."

"Hey! Look at that bridge!" Misty shouted. I'd swear it was the same bridge as the first one we crossed on our adventure. On the other hand, the second bridge we crossed looked just like it as well.

"Look! There's a food truck stopped for us to go by. Remember the hot breakfast the diner fixed for us and it stayed hot all night. See? That's the kind of impossible thing I'm talking about that makes me believe I'm dreaming," I declared.

"Even with our waitress and the cook in the front seat and turning to follow our caravan?" Misty said. In the rearview mirror, I saw the diner food truck turn to join our caravan.

"Do you suppose they are part of Hakuryū's circus?" I asked.

"Well, they're certainly a part of yours."

We rode on quietly except for Roadkill and Shasta singing for another fifteen minutes.

"The TripTik says turn left into the campground ahead."

I spotted it this time and was able to slow down and turn in. Déjà vu all over again.

"Misty, we've been going in a big circle! This is the same campground where we spent our first night. And there's site 33 with my symbol on it!" I pulled into the site and watched all the others in our caravan pull in with us. Freedom maneuvered his wagon into the next site over. I wouldn't need to walk far to get there. *Mmmhmm!*

IT HAD APPARENTLY been some time since Hakuryū's band of merry circus performers had been on the road together. It took a while to get everyone set up and I spent time wandering around to meet others. Even Freedom had to be instructed by Jeeves in how to set up the wagon. I walked over to the food truck and discovered they were pulling a little camper behind it. Sure enough, my waitress from the Diner was there, along with the cook who had fixed our magic breakfast. As soon as she saw me, the waitress rushed over to give me a hug. Yes, she did have a very nice shape and I might have held her a second or two longer than necessary.

"It is so wonderful to see you again, Warrior Wizard. Will you please join us for dinner? Bernard is fixing your favorite chili burger," she said. As far as she knew, it must be the only thing I eat, but it did sound good.

"I'll gladly join you," I said, "but you must call me Jackie."

"Of course, War... Jackie. I'm Raquel and my man over there is Bernard."

"In that case, may I bring my friends for dinner? You remember Misty and Roadkill. We've added Shasta and Princess and Freedom. Wait until you see him. He's so yummy!" I said.

"Oh, we'll serve the whole camp tonight," Bernard said, coming up to us. "I'd better start cooking." In a few minutes, half a dozen picnic tables had been moved to the area around the food truck. Camp was set up, music had begun from somewhere, and Raquel was hustling food from the truck to the company. I, naturally, managed to grab hold of my man and watch Raquel's eyes pop open when she saw him. She ran back to the truck and had an animated conversation with Bernard. A few minutes later, she returned with our meals. We both had the smothered chili burgers, but Freedom's plate was fully twice the size of mine!

"May I join you?" asked a voice I found slightly familiar. I turned and looked up at Scarecrow, the fixer.

"Hey! Please join us," I said. "You remember Misty, don't you? And Roadkill. This is Princess and Shasta, and this hunk beside me is Freedom."

"A pleasure to meet you all," he said as he sat. Raquel was there almost instantly with his dinner.

"What brings you back this way?" I asked.

"Waiting to join you for the trip to East Love," he said. "Word has gone out across the land for the big Succession Day celebration. It's very interesting. Some say it will be the reaffirmation of Baron Rex as the successor. Others say there will be an announcement of the marriage of Princess Rex. Still others say Valentine Caesar will be named as successor. Regardless, people are migrating from all over the land to East Love for the celebration."

"If we've done our job correctly, none of those will be correct," I said. "We've had a long and difficult road to follow these past weeks. I'm seeing it through to the end."

"The faithful discharge of your quest might still require action on your part," Scarecrow said. "Don't count the task as over yet."

"That's encouraging."

"What should we be expecting?" Misty asked.

"You've thwarted most of the incompetent plans of Valentine Caesar," Scarecrow said. "I know you've met him on numerous occasions. But he was never the brains of his family. His grandfather, August Caesar, hatched the plot to remove the Rex's line of succession. He's quite a powerful wizard himself. He would put Valentine on the throne, but by no means would the incompetent idiot actually rule. August intends to make the rules and collect the taxes."

"I've heard about him, but have only encountered his grandson."

"And you know you have to pass his fortress—I mean hotel resort—on the way into East Love. I would expect that someplace between here and there, you will meet his forces," Scarecrow said.

"Forces? Like an army?" Misty asked.

"Probably not that disciplined, nor that numerous, but just as determined."

"How do you know all this?" Princess asked.

"Ah, Princess. You know that when your brother was taken, his nanny was left on the swing set singing 'Swing Low, Sweet Chariot.' I was called to see about fixing her. Ultimately, I discovered she was actually in on the whole thing and when we got through the artificial barrier, she proved most informative about what was planned," Scarecrow said.

WE TALKED UNTIL nightfall, but everyone was tired from rushing to get on the road and drive the 200 miles we had today. Journeying in a caravan of circus wagons is a bit slower than it would be to just drive the distance in the Fairlane. We all retired early. I glanced in at my tent where Misty and Princess were settling down with the animals. When Roadkill saw me zipping up the tent from the outside, he hurriedly pushed his way out to join me. Well, he'd been with me the night before when I first met Freedom. It was always nice to know a dog was lying across the entrance.

I met Freedom at the door to the giant's wagon and he ushered me inside with Roadkill. What a beautiful little apartment! It had a higher ceiling than the other wagons so Freedom could stand up without danger of hitting his head. Everything was super-sized, including a more than king size bed. We soon discovered we could both stretch out fully on it and not have our feet hanging over the edge.

And, as soon as we could arrange ourselves, that was where we stayed for the rest of the night.

Chapter 13

The Last Battle

MILE 1671

FOR HAVING SUCH a celebratory atmosphere among the caravan, we managed to get a reasonable start to the day. I nearly didn't let Freedom get out of bed, but Misty came knocking at our door and called us to breakfast. I suppose I was still a little red in the face as everyone seemed to look our way and smile knowingly. Well, what of it? I was truly happy for the first time on this whole trip.

Not that I'd been particularly unhappy. Except when I killed a robber, and snapped the head off a snake in the middle of a thunderstorm, and faced down an ogre, and fought off four guys trying to walk off with Misty, damage my car, and kidnap Princess. Anyway, there was always Pepe's Tacos. That was good.

Ah, well. I was happy now.

We got in our cars and trucks and headed out of the campground after doing a thorough job of policing the area for trash and restoring picnic tables to their respective sites. As usual, Misty, Princess, and I led, with Shasta and Roadkill watching the road. Scarecrow had mounted Freedom's cab and was riding with him.

We were familiar with this part of the road since we drove it just two or three weeks ago. I was scanning the sky for thunder clouds. I definitely didn't want to be caught out in one of the mountain monster's attacks. We passed the barn, though it looked like just an abandoned farm and not the treaty shelter we had taken refuge in. On the other hand, my WW with a flaming basketball was painted on the side. There was still no sign of a storm, so we pressed on.

"Hey, aren't we about to the gas and coffee stop?" I asked. Misty scrambled to get the TripTik open just as we pulled over to pass a big tractor and wagon with a couple of dozen people riding on it. I recognized Little Lukey, proudly wearing his snakeskin belt and his wooden sword. Sure enough, Old Amos was driving the tractor and waved at us, falling in at the end of the caravan.

"Oh, my gosh!" Misty exclaimed. "The TripTik is full of annotations. Most of them say things like 'Caution!' or 'Keep Moving!' or some such. There are three places marked 'Possible Ambush!' I should have been watching the map all along!"

"What about the gas stop?" I demanded.

"It's marked about ten miles up with a note that says 'Circle the wagons!' What do you suppose that means?" Misty asked.

"I'd say it means we're about to get attacked. Possibly from all sides." I picked up speed a little and stuck an arm out my window to motion the caravan forward a little faster. I didn't dare move too fast because we had that tractor and wagon full of the McCoys at the tail end. I pulled over into the left lane so I could see the length of the caravan. We were stretched out way too far. "Roll down your window and motion Freedom forward, Misty!"

I barked. She complied and in a second Freedom was leaning out the window to get instructions.

"Move ahead and circle the wagons at the convenience store five miles ahead!" Misty shouted. "Pick up speed and get everyone secure and inside the circle." I'm sure Freedom shouted something back, but I couldn't understand it. He picked up speed and Misty repeated her instructions to Mr. Hakuryū. I didn't want to fall back too far or too fast, but I'd seen something that I didn't want to leave any of our people to face. Six dark vehicles were gaining on us. I was going to get in trouble for this, but it was the only thing I had that might slow them down.

I've often heard the expression that the lead vehicle of a convoy goes twenty miles per hour. The last vehicle in the convoy goes sixty in order to catch up. Unfortunately, we had our slowest vehicle at the end of the column and by the time Amos got the message and opened his tractor up as fast as it would go, the black vehicles were closing on us and we still had two miles to go to the convenience store. As soon as Amos was clear and a hundred yards away, I spun the wheel hard and brought the Fairlane into the lane facing back the direction we'd been going. I slammed it into reverse and started backwards as I fished a bean out of my pocket. I could see now they were black SUVs and were just fifty yards behind us. I threw the bean.

"Éclater!" I shouted. I fished another bean out, not knowing how big of an explosion I'd get. The blast put a good-sized hole in the middle of the road and one of the vehicles tipped nose down into it. Another slammed into it from behind, but four managed to swerve around the crater and continue pursuit. I threw again.

"Fumée!" I yelled. Smoke filled my field of vision and I heard brakes being slammed on as I threw another. "Mur de pierre!" There was a satisfying crunch as at least one vehicle emerged from the smoke to run smack into a stone wall. I spun the car around again and quickly caught up with Amos as he pulled into the convenience store gas station. I noticed there were two trucks with campers pulling horse trailers. Hunter and his people were unloading the horses into the circle for safety as well. With ten vehicles, we were able to make a pretty solid wall from the corners of the convenience store around the pumps. Dale and Og rushed out of the garage and once they saw us, went straight to work helping the children into the store. That included the dozen kids who had already descended on us with brushes and hoses and were reluctant to leave them without washing our vehicles. Misty convinced them that we'd all like a car wash once the shooting stopped.

Shooting. Dang! I hoped not, but I reached into the car glove box and pulled out the pistol that should still have six silver bullets in it. I also grabbed my basketball. Seeing what I had, Freedom grabbed his from the back of his truck.

We were just in time. Only two of the banged up black SUVs made it through, but they'd collected all their men. Then, from the other direction, we saw nearly a dozen more headed toward us.

Roadkill in his blue vest and spiked collar, and Shasta in her green boots prowled back and forth watching what was happening, shepherding an errant child back into the store, and welcoming the townspeople who came into our circle through the store, toting shotguns and pitchforks. In front of us were at least fifty men in black getting ready to move forward.

FORTUNATELY, NO ONE was trigger-happy. In fact, I wasn't sure some of the shotguns I saw had ever been fired. But as I looked at the men in black arrayed before us, it didn't look like they had any firearms. They were rather aimlessly milling about trying to decide what to do now that they were here. It seemed for the most part as if they simply expected people to surrender to their visage of authority.

"Give us the Rex brats and the rest of you can go on your merry way!" Valentine finally called from behind a couple of his men. "You have two minutes to comply!"

"Or what?" I yelled back.

"Or face the consequences."

"Come on, Valentine. You need to do better than that. We've gone pretty easy on you so far and you're still all battered up. Your three stooges are no longer with you. Have you told all your loyal retainers there what happened to them? One missing an eye. One with a hole in his gut. One with the side of his head burned off. That's what awaits those who attack us," I yelled. A lot of the guys with Valentine were looking strangely at him and several backed up behind the cars.

"You can't stand against us," Valentine promised.

"We'll wait," I said.

"Really? You should just give up, Warrior Wizard. You are trying to stand against the whole of Caesar's armies! The Great August Caesar has sent me to claim what is rightfully mine!" Valentine shouted.

"Not that impressive yet," I said. "Tell me, Valentine; do you have any children?"

"No! I'm only nineteen!"

"It's not all that likely that you'll see twenty. Who inherits the sovereignty when you die?"

"Why would I die?" he asked. It sounded like he'd genuinely never considered the option.

"There's a fifty-fifty chance that you'll die in the defeat of Caesar's armies today. I've instructed everyone to aim at you first. Eventually, people will stop shielding you and you'll run away, if you aren't dead. If by some miracle, you survive this battle, you'll be executed by the sovereign for treason. If you should ever manage to ascend the throne, someone near and dear to you will poison you. Basically, the only way to be reasonably sure you'll see your next birthday is to call off Caesar's armies and leave us alone," I said calmly.

He was getting nervous and kept looking skyward as if he were waiting for air support. I looked up and quickly saw what was happening. We were in the midst of a solar eclipse. The movie versions that show a dark shadow crossing the orb of the sun are a bunch of hooey. During a full eclipse, it doesn't really get noticeably darker until the sun is almost fully occluded. That point, however, was coming near. People were getting nervous. I was afraid everyone would panic when it suddenly got dark.

I didn't know the half of it.

We could feel the coolness and the shadow covering the sun only a second before a black shape swooped out of the sky and broke into half a dozen shapes—people in long black capes with fiery eyes and long front teeth rushing toward us.

"Vampires? Seriously?" I said. I didn't hesitate. I pulled out my gun, drew a bead on the lead vampire and pulled the trigger. I hit center mass with a silver bullet and it became a gaping hole with an expanding ring of smoke that consumed the entire vampire. It vanished in a last wisp. I drew down on the next vampire.

"NO! Stop! We'll leave!" the next vampire screeched. She turned and hissed at Valentine as the remaining vampires coalesced and flew away.

We didn't really have time to fully appreciate the victory as Caesar's army moved forward. They were met by another horde sweeping up out of the ground. The apparitions appeared so quickly that the army was taken completely by surprise.

"Sorry we're late," Raymond said from beside me. I turned and saw the ghost hotel manager and Joan, his chef daughter. Flooding toward the army were all the ghosts of Amherst. "We had to wait until dark to have the ghosts appear."

"Where is the noise coming from?" I asked. Screeches and howls and a sound of rushing wind accompanied a noxious odor that was mostly focused in front of us, but I could still catch a whiff.

"You taught us. We recorded all kinds of effects and developed some odors we could use. Unfortunately, all the villagers will disappear when the eclipse fades, so we only have about five minutes."

It was enough time for half the army to desert and six SUVs peeled out, headed back the way we'd come.

THE SCREECHING AND the ghosts faded. The locals, the circus people, the treaty barn people and the rest all looked at me with a sense of wonder. The first battle was over. Of course, we knew there would be another strike from Valentine, but I rather thought he'd thrown his best at us with the vampires.

I was surprised that there had been no shots fired other than the one I used. I knew Valentine had a gun and I expected that his gang was the kind to hide behind maximum firepower. Somehow, I needed to get him tied up as quickly as possible. I heard a rhythmic beat to my right and looked to see Freedom bouncing a basketball. An idea came to me. I started bouncing my ball as well. We picked up a rhythm together and Hunter's people pulled drums out of their trucks and picked up the beat. One of the circus people brought a big bass drum out and joined the rhythm.

It seems like there is always one would-be berserker in a crowd. While one group of people runs away, this one person gets hyper mad and decides to take on everyone himself. It looked like Valentine was egging his berserker on. The remaining army was falling in behind him and they were ready to charge.

At the first step, I flung my basketball with all my strength at the big bad guy. When it hit his forehead, it burst into flames, taking off all his hair in an instant. Must be using some kind of hair oil the way it went up like a torch. Freedom passed me another basketball as mine bounced back toward him. He snatched it out of the air one-handed and picked up the rhythm of the dribble. I put the second ball into the air, slamming a guy who was trying to sneak up on the outside corner. The big berserker advanced again. Freedom kept feeding me basketballs, but this guy was going to take some more power. I dipped my hand into my pouch and pulled out Roadkill's ball.

I love the sound of the crack of the bat. This time, though, it was the berserker's head that met the ball. Roadkill was in action at once, picking the bouncing ball out of the air and trotting back to the circle. This time the behemoth dropped like a rock. Two buddies grabbed his body and stuffed it in the back of an SUV. Three more jumped into the car with them and took off south—the direction of their friends' retreat. I picked off another with a basketball. Somehow, Freedom was picking up all the rebounds and kept passing me balls, all the while maintaining the beat.

On one side, the local farmers, including Amos and his clan, had gone out to meet a flank of the attackers with pitchforks and clubs. Off to my right, Princess was in a sword fight with a guy who had all he could do to defend himself against her vicious attack. I tried to keep an eye on her, but was being pressed on one side by another guy with a sword. And on the other by a guy with a knife. The stole came off my shoulders and became a double ended sword with the handle in the middle. I knew this sword was insanely sharp as I'd sliced a werewolf in half with it.

The battle was short. They both attacked at the same time as I spun the sword in my hands. It made contact with both the knife and the sword at the same time and severed the blades. The two guys looked in disbelief at the handles they were holding, dropped them, and ran. The swordsman who had been battling Princess lost his weapon and joined the retreat. Two cars left the scene and the other combatants were falling back to their cars for cover. I saw Valentine dive for a car and it turned north toward East Love.

"Stop that car!" I yelled. The last three cars were revving engines, but looked like they planned to ram the circle of wagons. I couldn't have that, even if shithead got away.

I plunged my hand into my pocket and pulled out the last three beans I had. I threw them at the cars. "Germer et pousser!" I shouted. I knew what I meant, but when they hit the ground under the three cars and sprouted, they looked awfully small. The cars started to move, but didn't get more than a foot before the beanstalks lifted them into the air. In seconds, the cars were twenty feet in the air and the occupants were scrambling to find a way out and down as they kept getting higher.

I turned to look after Valentine and saw he, too, had not made it far. Og, the mountain ogre, had hold of the back bumper and it was lifted two feet off the ground as he dragged the car back to the gas station with its wheels spinning. Dale was quick with a set of jack stands to put under the axle of the car so it wouldn't move, no matter how fast they spun the wheels. As Og set the car down, she put chocks in front and behind the front tires.

"Nice job, Og," I said as I stepped up to him.

"Help Warrior Wizard," he said, nodding. Oh, well. I had a feeling Dale didn't want him for his scintillating conversation. I walked around the car until I spotted Valentine and tried to open his door. The coward had locked all the doors and was scrambling to get his gun loaded and ready. I didn't have time to waste, so I whipped the stole off and swung it through the door frame, severing it. The door fell off and Valentine swung the gun around, just in time to be met by the gold cord circling his body.

"Drop it!" I commanded. The gun fell to the ground. Valentine looked scared. Freedom stepped up to one side of me and Og to the other. I'd guess that was a pretty menacing sight for a fellow who couldn't be more than five-ten. I led Valentine into the circle of wagons and let the locals figure out how to deal with the car on blocks and the three on beanstalks. "I want you to obey me and give up this ridiculous drive to become the Sovereign," I started.

"I can't," he said. I could tell he was struggling to do what I wanted him to under the cord of submission, but something else was stronger. "Grandfather put a compulsion on me and I can't fight it off." Well, that was crap. Now what was I going to do?

"Scarecrow!" I hollered.

"At your service, Warrior Wizard," he said from nearby. Freedom moved aside and I could see the fixer.

"We have a problem here. Maybe you can fix it. Poor Valentine was placed under a compulsion by his grandfather to seek to become sovereign. That means, we can never let him go unless you can fix him," I said.

"Let me see what I can do. He's under duress right now. Do you have a cord that will bind him without making him submit?"

As a matter of fact, I did have. I quickly wrapped the blue cord around him and removed the gold. He immediately began to breathe more easily.

"Now, Valentine," Scarecrow said, placing an arm around the boy, "do you really want to be your grandfather's puppet in this?"

"No, sir. I was in college, but when I came home for the summer, Grandfather August put me in a trance and planted a compulsion to become the Sovereign elect. I just want to go back to college and party," Valentine said. I got the feeling he didn't really care about college if he could just party.

When Scarecrow started with probing questions, like, "How long has your grandfather been abusing you?" I left

Valentine bound with my cord for what I assumed was going to be a long counseling session. I found Og and Dale escorting the men from Valentine's car to a holding area.

"Dale, what's the chance of getting a latte? Looks like we could be here a while."

"No problem, Warrior Wizard. Misty is already at the bar pulling shots. Now that we have this car empty, Og can take care of it and I'll go help her," Dale said. She stripped off her coveralls and was suddenly the miniskirted barista that everyone naturally followed.

"Warrior Wizard Jackie, we can't stop for long," Princess said as she and her brother and Hakuryū approached. "Tomorrow is Succession Day and we need to be home for the ceremony."

"According to our log book, there is only another 150 miles to East Love. If we camp here for the night, we can still get up and be in East Love by mid-morning."

"Cutting it tight, aren't you, Warrior Wizard?" Hakuryū said. We looked over where the local fire department had a ladder truck propped up to the first beanstalk with a car on top. The black suits were filing down the ladder from the car, trying to keep their hands up.

"I think it's a rule of quests. You have to arrive just before it's too late," I said. "Even if we weren't there, we have Valentine. There's no other candidate for the succession, so they won't do anything about removing Baron."

"Warrior Wizard," Joan approached me, all excited. "Rachel and Bernard are going to let me cook in their kitchen truck. I get to serve dinner."

"That's wonderful. Will the town ghosts be able to join us?" I asked.

"With your permission," Raymond said.

"Yes, of course. If they can travel with us all the way to East Love, we can do a big promotion for the ghost town resort!" I said. I really loved the ghosts.

"Can we wash your car?" an urchin asked from beside me. She handed me a fresh latte. I took a sip and smiled. Heavenly.

"Wash mine and anyone else who wants it," I said. "And have Dale check the gas and oil for everyone when she gets a break." The kids dragged hoses, buckets, and sponges over to my car and started in on it. I glanced over to where the guys were being rounded up from the beanstalk cars. They were cowering against a fire truck. Shasta was prancing back and forth in front of them with a mama bobcat and two more cubs backing her up. Whenever anyone moved, a large black bear roared at him.

I reacted before I even knew what was happening. I snatched my basketball out of the air with my right hand and began to dribble. I looked where it had come from and Freedom was grinning at me. He pointed to the corner of the building where a basketball backboard and hoop hung. I launched the ball from where I was and dropped it through the hoop. Freedom grabbed it and spun it back to me. Before I started dribbling, I dropped my gown at my feet and we were off and running.

What a great feeling to be working up a sweat doing something I loved to do. With someone I loved! I knew very well it was too soon to feel as strongly about Freedom as I did. I was just going to get my heart broken when I woke up. Maybe... Just maybe this wasn't a dream.

Freedom scored on me. I needed to get my head back in the game.

It wasn't exactly like the first time we played. I didn't jump up and wrap my legs around him and ride him to the ground. But it was two hot and sweaty people who dragged themselves into his wagon and got a good hot shower together. And a nap. And stuff.

SCARECROW WAS WAITING for me when I emerged from Freedom's wagon. Responsibilities, I suppose.

"How goes the repair work?" I asked the fixer.

"It's not exactly something *I* can fix," he sighed.

"Damn! Am I going to have to keep him tied up until after the Succession Day celebration?" I asked.

"I don't think so. His grandfather was a sneaky one. He held out a hope for Valentine to be free of the compulsion on one condition."

"I'm dying to hear."

"The same thing that you got: Love's first kiss," Scarecrow said as if it was as easy as getting a loaf of bread from the convenience store. He looked at me and raised an eyebrow.

"No. Oh, no you don't. Like you said, I got mine and I'm not giving it away to anyone else. No no no no. I am not kissing any frogs."

The damned guy started laughing at me. I realized I'd been played and I was not happy about it. I just shook my head and bared my teeth at him.

"I don't think you'll need to worry about it," he said. He pointed to where Dale had gone to release one of the prisoners. The guy immediately ran toward Valentine. I recognized him. Hard not to. I was the one who poked his eye out. He'd changed to a black patch over it instead of the huge bandage that he had worn. He had an intense conversation with his boss and I turned to Scarecrow.

"Is that wise? That's got to be his number one hench-man, assuming I killed the other two. They could be plotting something," I said.

"I'm sure they are," Scarecrow answered. Just then, One-eye darted in and placed a kiss right on Valentine's lips. He pulled away and the two of them looked at each other, then around them guiltily. Seeing no one paying attention, they moved into a clinch with an eye-opening kiss. "True love's first kiss," Scarecrow said. "His grand-father was certain no woman would willingly have his grandson. And the boy had shown no interest in women at all. He just hadn't admitted that he was attracted to Juan. It was the injury to Juan that made him realize how important his friend was to him. I guess, in a round-about way he can thank you for true love's first kiss after all."

"Well, I'll be! Good for him! Good for them! You really think this will break the compulsion?"

"Only one way to find out. Let's go have a conversation."

The conversation was good. Valentine and Juan put their hands on the pommel of my sword and swore they would never seek the sovereignty again.

"We're going to head south tomorrow, if you'll permit it," Juan said.

"We can get married in Adavenia. I'm never going to let this guy out of my sight again," Valentine said. We went around to the other prisoners and with the judicious application of the gold cord of submission, all pledged they would support the ascension of Princess to the Sovereignty.

I was pretty sure I hadn't actually killed anyone in the battle of the gas station. Except one poor vampire. Oops. Sorry about that.

Chapter 14

Journey's End

YOU WOULD SCARCELY KNOW there had been a battle the next morning. A crane had removed the SUVs from the tops of the beanstalks and the stalks themselves had been cut down and pieces were sold as souvenirs. There was even a figurine of me that had been carved from the woody stem. How sweet. A road crew had been out to repair the damage I'd done to the highway trying to stop Valentine and his crew. You'd never see that kind of rapid response and repair work in the real world. That should convince anyone I was dreaming. But the hunk whose arm I was holding had done his best to convince me I wasn't dreaming the previous night.

Traffic was the heaviest I'd seen since coming to Victoriana. A steady stream of cars passed the convenience store gas station hardware grocery espresso stand. We moved the wagons to stage ourselves to move out and give people access to the gas pumps and store. Dale was inside pulling shots of coffee with Misty's assistance. Amos led our group out of the parking area and put on all speed to join the traffic to East Love. His tractor and hay wagon were the slowest vehicle in our procession. We had a lot of debate regarding who should go next and ended up with Hunter's tribe following with their horse trailers. Then Misty jumped into the car and I led the circus wagons out in my Fairlane. The last in line were the diner truck and the ghost car. The ghosts would all arrive after dark, but Raymond and Joan were driving. Dale and Og said they would catch up in a few hours. We crossed the bridge and headed out of the little hamlet toward East Love.

With the speed of our convoy and necessary stops for animals and humans to relieve themselves, it took a long time to reach the festival.

MILE 1814

IN FACT, IT was nearly dinner time when our convoy wound its way into town and circled the palace grounds. After making one full trip around the structure, which I was sure had once been a county courthouse, I pulled in to the portico where Regis and Regina Rex were standing on the steps. Mr. Hakuryū followed in his circus wagon while Freedom parked on the street. The rest of the convoy was parked around the square and were already setting up various acts with acrobats and jugglers. The food truck must have been cooking on the entire journey from the convenience store. Raquel and Bernard were serving food out the side of the truck as quickly as they could. Amos and his clan were set up for a square dance on one side of the grounds while Hunter and his tribe created a village on the other side and gave kids horseback rides.

And those were only the acts and people who were in our convoy. Dozens of booths and acts were set up on or near the grounds. Somehow, Joan and Raymond had set up an entire dining room area in the street and were advertising a 'Dine with the Ghosts' adventure, starting at nightfall.

Misty, Princess, and I got out of the Fairlane with Roadkill and Shasta taking up positions on either side of us. We met Mr. Hakuryū and Baron as they got out of their truck. Freedom and Scarecrow joined us as well. I bowed to the Sovereign and swept off my mortarboard.

"Your Sovereignty, I am pleased to return to you in the company of your children, Princess Bridget Rex and Baron Federico Rex. Accompanying us on this trip are the giant Freedom, the fixer Scarecrow, and the dragon Mr. Hakuryū, as well as my companions, Misty, Roadkill, and Shasta," I said with all the formality I could muster.

"As promised, Wizard Warrior Jackie, you shall be rewarded up to half the sovereign lands of Victoriana for returning the jewel of our crown to us," the sovereign said. He swept down the stairs to embrace his son.

"Not so fast, Dad," Baron said. "Jackie has been a kind escort and bodyguard, but it was my sister Princess Bridget Rex, who rescued me by defeating the dragon in the Last Battle. Therefore, it is Princess who deserves the reward of half the sovereignty. And in grateful appreciation of her heroism, I, Baron Federico Rex, heir to the sovereign and established successor, grant to Princess Bridget Rex the other half of our sovereignty that the Land might be united under her beneficence."

I was pretty sure Hakuryū had coached him on that speech. I wondered what they'd been doing on the journey.

"You walked right into that one, Ferdinand," Pop said.

Pop!? My head snapped away from the family reunion and up a step to where Mam and Pop were standing. Misty and I rushed them to give them a big hug.

"What are you doing here?" I asked. "And how did you get here?"

"Well, hello to you, too," Mam said. "What kind of greeting was that?"

"I mean... I'm so happy to see you, but I'm so confused! I never expected to see you in my dream."

"Dream? You aren't dreaming, girl," Pop said. "We got here by one of the usual ways. Over the mountain pass with a stop at the diner for a chili burger and fries. Then we drove straight here. What you were supposed to do."

"But how do you know the Rexes?" I pressed.

"Oh, Mam and I met them years ago, when we were on the great motorcycle rally around the country."

"But that was like... a long time ago. Were Regis and Regina babies?"

"No, no, no. Nothing like that. Time just moves at a different pace here than it does back home. Why, next time you chance to arrive here, you'll have aged by the time you were away and the people here will scarcely seem to have aged at all."

That made me stop and think. First, it seemed to be expected that I'd leave the Land and go back to our reality. Second, no matter how long I stayed away, when I came back, people here would scarcely have aged. I reached back and felt Freedom's reassuring hand in mine.

"Mam, Pop, I'd like you to meet my boyfriend, Freedom. We met a few days ago, but I've fallen head over heels in love."

"Oh, dear," Mam said. "Oh! It's nice to meet you, Freedom. This complicates things. Very complicated."

"Friends, we need to go make things official and let people start partying," Regis said. "Come and join us on the stage for the succession ritual."

THE FANFARE THAT welcomed us sounded a lot bigger than the dozen or twenty instruments I could see clustered together. The sovereign's short minion, Clark, hurried us over to where we were to walk up the aisle to the platform on which Baron and Princess's parents and my grandparents were waiting. Misty and I flanked Baron and Princess with Roadkill and Shasta beside us and Freedom and Hakuryū behind us. The three armorers— Tomas, Renee, and Oscar—who had outfitted us before the adventure rushed up to us with brushes and damp cloths to clean our clothes as we stood there. I personally thought Renee spent a little too much time making sure Freedom's chest and stomach were clean.

Then it was time to process to the front.

You know that last scene in the original Star Wars where Han, Luke, Chewy, R2-D2, and C-3PO get their big reward and the band plays. Well, George Lucas got it right. He just hung medals on their necks and everyone applauded. Run the credits. The reality was not nearly as fun. I swear that Regis spoke for half an hour about the Land and its friends from the other side. He spoke of the importance of unity and kindness in going forward. He scarcely mentioned the kidnapping and the Caesars' attempt to usurp the throne. I noted, however, that a gaunt man not far away looked plenty upset and furtively looked around. I began fingering my cords as I watched him and almost missed bending down to get my own medal hung around my neck.

Then there was the big investiture and transfer, making Princess the sovereign-elect. Regis also announced his support for Freedom's quest to return to his mother with Hakuryū and his granting of the request of his daughter and son to go with them. Nothing was mentioned about me.

Finally, we cleared the stage and various acts took over entertaining. Raymond and Joan announced the opening of the Dine with a Ghost adventure and I took Freedom and Misty and the animals over to where they were set up so we could have dinner.

It was quite lovely, even though I wasn't sure where Joan was doing her cooking. People saw the Warrior Wizard dining with the ghosts and flocked to the improvised dining room. It looked like they would be very successful. In another part of the festival, Hunter's minstrel was singing the Ballad of the Warrior Wizard after which Little Luke told of his adventure on Thunder Mountain. Just then, another man stepped up and told an equally riveting tale about the battle with the werewolves and I recognized hapless Charlie. There was another verse of the ballad.

But people weren't finished embarrassing me. Dale told the story of the taming of the ogre and punctuated it by kissing the big oaf. Then there was the basketball battle with the giant, followed by the Last Battle at the convenience store. With each telling, the stories were embellished a little more until you wouldn't have recognized the actual event from the ballad that was being sung.

The revelers partied late into the night. It was well after midnight when I was finally able to slip into the wagon with my giant.

I WOKE UP suddenly at about 3:30 in the morning. Freedom was breathing deep and easy. But I had a sudden feeling that things weren't right. I slipped out of bed, careful not to disturb my boyfriend, and pulled on my cap and gown, belting on my sword and dagger. Ever so quietly, I opened the door to the wagon and slipped out into the darkness. Even Roadkill, lying across the doorway, didn't stir. I tried to count back however many days it had been since the full moon werewolf battle, but lost track. Either we were in the dark phase or it hadn't risen yet. Regardless, it was black as pitch out. That made me wonder where the streetlights were. There had been lots of light all evening. I looked over toward where the ghost party had been and could see faint shapes of them hovering motionless in the air. Something was definitely wrong.

I started working my way around the perimeter of the large square and saw the playground from which Baron had initially been abducted. It looked normal, but one swing was rocking back and forth as if someone had just left it. At the corner of the square, where there was a cannon, the two policemen who were honor guards were slumped over.

I scooted on around the building, as a fog began to creep in from all around the square. I hurried toward my car, still parked with Mr. Hakuryū's wagon under the buidling's portico. And there I saw him: The gaunt figure I'd earlier identified as August Caesar. He was just standing up from putting something under my car. Then he turned to the front door of the palace, raised his arms, and started chanting.

No good could come of this. I needed to break up whatever spell he was working on. I didn't have my bas-ketball, but Roadkill's ball was in my pouch. I gripped it firmly and let it fly as if I were pegging it from first to third. It hit him, but he shrugged it off as if it were a fly that buzzed him. I pulled my slingshot out and began firing clay pellets at him, watching them bounce off some kind of invisible wall surrounding him. Still, he was chanting and the fog was getting closer. I needed to get closer and get personal. I reached for a bean, but I'd used the last of them at the gas station. Instead, I felt the feather Tomas had given me. What the hell could I do with a feather? Then I thought that so far, I'd been trying to attack and was just bouncing off as he kept chanting. I needed to distract him.

I held the feather in the palm of my hand and blew softly toward Caesar.

"Chatouiller," I whispered. The feather drifted toward the wizard and slipped silently through his wards. It started with his ears. I saw him twitch a little, but he didn't break off the chant. The feather circled his neck and he shrugged his shoulders, but still chanted. The fog was almost to us now. I urged the feather on. It crept up from beneath his chin and began to tickle his nose. It took a moment as he struggled to keep chanting and then suddenly sneezed. The fog drifted back as if blown by his sternutation. He jerked around toward me and the wards fell away. I started toward him but a gesture had me fighting against a wall of gelatin.

"You can't stop me with your little tricks. Everyone is asleep and I will drag both brats out of the palace and take them away with me. No Rex will ever see the throne in Victoriana again!" he declared. I'd had about enough of this guy. I stepped back and the wall loosened around me. I drew my sword and dagger as he reached for the door handle. I sliced forward and felt the gelatin give way before the sword of truth. And with the next swing, it sliced through his extended hand.

He howled in rage and pain and swung the other hand toward me, a flaming sword in it. I didn't hesitate. I sliced off the other hand and it and the sword both fell to the ground. The fog was fleeing now and lights were coming on in the square. The old man was not to be thwarted so easily. He began flailing at me with his bloody stumps and I couldn't help but think of the black knight in Monty Python and the Holy Grail. 'It's just a scratch. I'll kick you!' I was whittling off pieces of his arm as he kept up his attack. And then he stopped and stared at me, his mouth open in a silent wail. His eyes looked down and I followed them to see his chest impaled on my dagger. August Caesar crumpled to the ground.

Lights! Camera! Action!

The entire square was suddenly bustling with activity. All the lights were on and soldiers who had only just been asleep on their cannons were rushing toward me. The ghosts were moving, doors were opening on wagons and in a moment the front doors of the palace were flung open and Regis stood staring at the ground. He looked in horror at the several pieces of August's arms, the still flaming sword guttering in the severed hand. He looked at the bloody weapons in my hands and said, "Arrest her!"

WELL, THANKS A whole shitload. I stop a madman from breaking into the palace and creating all kinds of havoc and chaos and they throw me in jail.

Actually, there wasn't any throwing involved. Unless I went over and stood in front of the cannon, there was no weapon the police could point at me. I unceremoniously wiped my sword and dagger on the old man's robes, sheathed them, and accompanied them to the dungeon. Outside, Freedom, Hakuryū, Og, and Amos were raising a hullaballoo. Roadkill was barking and finally broke through to trot alongside me as we went down near where we'd been armed and outfitted just a few weeks ago.

Roadkill walked right into the cell with me and they closed the door behind us. I stretched out on the bed and went to sleep with Roadkill lying beside me. The next time I woke up, I was determined to wake up for real. I give them all this help and get a medal for a reward and save them from the evil wizard trying to break into the palace and they throw me in jail. Heck with 'em!

Unfortunately, I woke up in jail when they brought breakfast to me. It was a good breakfast and I thought I detected Bernard's hand in how hot the food was and how flavorful and filling. I'd met the palace chef once on my first visit to East Love and he made a fine meal. Joan had cooked an excellent breakfast at the ghost hotel. Mr. Hakuryū's cook had made a terrific breakfast. But nothing quite compared to the breakfast Bernard had sent with us from the diner that was still hot and fresh when we ate it the next morning.

I ate and drank the coffee, feeding bits to Roadkill, even though he had his own dish. I kept thinking I heard voices, but no one came near my cell. I'd finished breakfast and the last of my coffee when the guard came to get me. He was accompanied by one of the kitchen staff who cleaned up my dishes on a cart and backed away from me carefully.

"Warrior Wizard, if you would please accompany me, the court is ready to convene. Please don't hurt me. I didn't want you put in jail. It was obvious to everyone that you'd broken some enchantment the old man was weaving."

"Don't worry. I've got no beef with you." It was pretty ridiculous that I had just spent a night in jail fully armed. I was still in my cap and gown with all the regalia. I had my sword and dagger, plus the slingshot and pellets. Roadkill was proudly carrying his ball. No one else was carrying any armament that I could detect, though August Caesar had done just fine with his hands and produced a flaming sword out of thin air.

As we climbed the stairs to the upper levels, the sound of voices became more pronounced. Loud, angry voices filled the atrium as a crowd was held back from rushing the palace. When I appeared, there was a loud cheer. Freedom broke through the ring of guards and dragged Misty with him to my side. Shasta leapt to Roadkill's back and rode in style. The guards didn't seem to care that my entourage was now complete, they were focused on seeing to it that no one else got through. We went up to the second floor and were ushered into a typical county courtroom. It could have come directly out of a Perry Mason TV show. I was led to the front left of the courtroom where Pop was waiting for me. The others slid into the first row of seats next to Mam.

"What the heck is going on here?" I asked Pop. "Why is the sovereign so upset?"

"If I were to guess, it would be that Caesar left some kind of geas on him," Pop said. "We need to break through it and open his eyes. He ate like an automaton at breakfast this morning."

"Great. Now the guy who wanted me here wants me put away. I'm ready to go back home," I pouted.

"Well, that's not exactly where you should go," Pop said. "Mam and I came to meet you and drive the rest of the way to Winston with you. We have your things and

Misty's packed in a U-Haul trailer so we can get you settled into your apartment before training camp starts."

"What? Training camp doesn't start until August. It's only, um... like the end of June? Right?" I suddenly wasn't sure what date it was.

"It's the whole time-distortion thing," Pop said. "You might have been here in the Land for only two or three weeks, but we left home two months after you did."

"That's bizarre."

The court came to order as the Sovereign entered and everyone stood. I thought it was strange that there was no one over at the prosecution's table. Just Pop and me at the defendant's table. We all sat down and the Sovereign rapped his gavel to call us to order. It was plain to see he wasn't himself.

"Prosecutor, read the charges!" he declared. There was no prosecutor present. The sovereign got up and came around to the front of the bench and read out the charges as if he were the prosecutor.

"On the day in question, while the entire town of East Love was in peaceful repose, the Wizard Warrior Jackie did confront and murder a random citizen of the town on the palace steps. We request the immediate imprisonment of the defendant for life."

"I object, your honor!" Pop said. We waited for the Sovereign to get back behind his desk as judge.

"Overruled," he said. "We declare the defendant guilty and sentence her to life in prison." There was a roar of outrage from the people in the courtroom with several standing and heading toward the bench. Shasta jumped to the table and hissed. We could hear an answering roar from the downstairs and it seemed to be getting closer.

"This is too much," I said. Pop tried to hold me back, but I stood and walked straight up to the bench. "You're under the influence of an evil wizard," I declared to the judge. "But you've chosen to convict me for having protected you and your family from one who wanted nothing more or less than to take your throne. Well, I've had enough." I slapped a piece of paper on the judge's desk and shouted, "Libérer!" My get out of jail free card.

"You can't do that! You have to go to jail. Something is wrong. Someone stop her. It's not right. I need to go to jail. Someone arrest me." The Sovereign was pretty much down to gibberish by the time we reached the doors of the courtroom. We headed down to the lobby where people started cheering like I was a long-lost savior instead of a just-released criminal. I was beyond caring. My car was still parked in front of the palace with Hakuryū's wagon behind. I turned to Freedom. And he pulled me into a hug the likes of which I wanted never to end.

"What now, Jackie?" he asked.

"I'm headed for college at Winston in Iowa. I have to report to basketball camp so I can be one of the Winston Warriors this winter. Just get in your truck and follow me out of here." I kissed him firmly.

"I can't do that," he said. I looked at him blankly. "I can't leave the Land and I've promised to return to my mother with Hakuryū. Can't you come with us?"

"If I stay in the Land any longer, I'll miss the whole school year, my scholarship, my opportunities. You have to come with me. You have to," I complained, knowing my words were futile. I kissed him again and turned to motion Misty and the animals into the car. That's when I saw the bundle lying under the wheel, smoking slightly.

I looked up at the Sovereign, babbling on the steps and wondered where Princess and Baron and Regina were. I scraped the bundle out from under the car with my toe and Regis focused on it, pointing. I could see others beginning to track the bundle. This could get bad.

I snatched the magnifying glass out of my bag and began to examine the bundle. It was tied up with a cord and the tendril of smoke was escaping through the tie. I'd read about this in the manual the first night—a horcrux. The wizard had transferred his soul into the bundle. It needed to be destroyed before he captured everyone in his power. And the answer was in my hand. A bright spot shone on the bundle where the magnifying glass focused the sunlight. I adjusted the distance to the bundle and the spot became hot. I cooked that little bundle with the sunlight and in a few minutes, it burst into flames and disintegrated.

I looked around. The people looked like they were just waking up. Regis sank down with a sigh. Suddenly Princess burst through the doors and ran to me, wrapping her arms around me.

"Thank you! Thank you, Warrior Wizard. It was terrible. We could see everything that was going on and couldn't do anything. Please don't hate father. He wasn't himself," she said. Regis was being propped up between two of his retainers. He waved at me.

"She's right. I could see what I was doing and I couldn't do anything about it. Thank you again for freeing us."

"Well, I'm afraid I still need to go," I said. Mam and Pop pulled up in front with the U-Haul behind their Fusion. "Are you sure, Freedom? Time runs differently out there. It could be years before I can come back."

"You conquered me and brought me back to life," he said. "I will always love you, Jackie the Beanstalk.

Always." He let me go and we piled into the Fairlane. Just Misty, Roadkill, and me again. I snapped my head back to the back seat again. And a bobcat kitten. Oh, life on the other side was still going to be interesting.

WE DROVE OVER the pass and down to the Land of Anatnomia, only there was no customs house or border crossing there. We headed south and pulled into a roadside taco restaurant called Pepe's. They had a good burrito.

"Don't you need gas?" Pop asked as we got ready to leave. I looked at the gauge. It was riding just above empty. Wow! Good thing he said something. While I filled the tank, I pulled off my cap and gown and grabbed a pair of shorts and T-shirt out of my backpack. We headed toward Iowa.

I was sad. I'd found true love and we belonged in different worlds. I didn't care about the magic or being a warrior wizard. Love! I'd found it and lost it. Misty turned on the radio and as we followed Mam and Pop, we sang along with the music.

> *Freedom's just another word for nothin' left to*
> *lose*
> *Nothin', and that's all that Bobby left me.*

I was already thinking about my return trip for the Christmas holidays. I wondered how much time would have passed. Apparently, it wasn't just a dream.

The End

www.ingramcontent.com/pod-product-compliance
Lightning Source LLC
Chambersburg PA
CBHW070615310726
48982CB00001B/91